GUNS ON THE HIGH MESA

**Center Point
Large Print**

**This Large Print Book carries the
Seal of Approval of N.A.V.H.**

GUNS ON THE HIGH MESA

Arthur Henry Gooden

CENTER POINT PUBLISHING
THORNDIKE, MAINE

This Center Point Large Print edition
is published in the year 2009 by arrangement with
Golden West Literary Agency.

Copyright © 1943 by Arthur Henry Gooden.
Copyright © 1948 under the title *High Mesa* by Arthur
Henry Gooden. Copyright © renewed 1971 by the
Estate of Arthur Henry Gooden.

The text of this Large Print edition is unabridged.
In other aspects, this book may vary
from the original edition.
Printed in the United States of America.
Set in 16-point Times New Roman type.

ISBN: 978-1-60285-421-5

Library of Congress Cataloging-in-Publication Data

Gooden, Arthur Henry, 1879-1971.
  Guns on the high mesa / Arthur Henry Gooden.
    p. cm.
  ISBN 978-1-60285-421-5 (library binding : alk. paper)
  1. Large type books. I. Title.

PS3513.O4767G86 2009
813'.52--dc22

2008047942

Affectionately inscribed to
MY SISTER
FANNY GOODEN PERKINS

Contents

1
Clouds

FROM where he lazily sprawled in the deep veranda chair young MacKenzie could see the timbered slopes of the Palos Verdes, dark against the clean blue of the Arizona sky. Farther down to the east lifted the rugged peaks of the San Franciscos, touched with fleecy cloud drift.

His weather-wise eyes appraisingly studied their upward push. He knew they were traveling at tremendous speed and that long before the noonday sun dipped below the horizon its hot glare would vanish under the cooling gray veil of welcome rain.

Storm MacKenzie was serenely certain of the signs. It was on such a day that his father once stood on this same wide veranda and anxiously scrutinized the distant peaks of the San Franciscos. Cattle were dying on the parched range, and like every Arizona rancher Jim MacKenzie was deeply interested in the portents. Prolonged drought threatened unthinkable disaster. His ambition to found an empire of cattle in the new territory of Arizona would wither with the thirsting grass.

Young MacKenzie's lean, sun-weathered face softened as he recalled his father's drawling voice telling of that day just thirty-two years past.

'Was feelin' awful low, son . . . waitin' for you to

be born, and watchin' the clouds hoverin' top of the Frisco peaks . . . wonderin' if she'd rain in time to save the grass . . . save the ranch—'

Jim MacKenzie's belief in the portents that on the same day brought rain to the range and the son to carry on his name was to become a tradition. 'Clouds smokin' over the Friscos' meant a sure prophecy of rain.

For hours he had watched the gathering storm, the dismal load of doubt and despair easing from wide, hard-muscled shoulders as the rain came slanting down like silver threads of newborn hope. Lightning ripped the heavens to the deep-toned rumble of thundering drums that sent tremors through the new little ranch-house. Perhaps Jim MacKenzie had valid reason to be slightly incoherent when he turned and stared at the blanket-wrapped bundle in the arms of the beaming Mexican woman who suddenly made a noiseless appearance through the open door.

She stood there, smiling at him, made soft little cooing sounds, a brown hand fluttering over the bundle cradled in her arms.

'What . . . *what is—it*, Ynes?'—Jim MacKenzie's voice was husky, scarce above a whisper.

The woman's answer came in soft Spanish, jubilant, exulting: 'Your son, señor . . . so strong a man he is already—'

Jim MacKenzie gazed at her, then lowered his look to the baby in her arms, and his hard brown features took on an odd paleness. Suddenly the color flowed back, and face upturned to the driving rain he solemnly said: 'I'm namin' him "Storm," for the storm came with him and with the storm came deliverance from ruin. I thank God for him and always will.'

Jim MacKenzie was gone, and the pioneer wife who had brought his man-child into the world that stormy day. The little ranch-house was grown into a large rambling structure, half-hidden among the trees planted in those years for the pleasure of the girl-bride who had come up with Jim from Texas with his herd of longhorns. They were tall trees by now, and the winds whispered ceaseless music through the pines that towered in kindly vigil above the graves of Jim and Lucy MacKenzie. The longhorns that once wore the Diamond M on their hides were gone, too. In their stead white-faced cattle roamed over the range Jim MacKenzie had wrested from an untamed wilderness.

The soft pad of sandaled feet swung the young cowman's gaze to the door. Ynes came slowly from the shadowed depths of the hall. She was plump, now, instead of slender, and her once black hair was white. Only her eyes remained the same, dark and lustrous and singularly intelligent. She came to a standstill in the doorway, stared intently at the man in the big porch chair.

Storm MacKenzie gave her a slow, quizzical smile. He knew the meaning of that brooding look.

11

'When your father was your age he had a son'—the Mexican woman's tone was reproachful.

'Give me time, Ynes,' drawled the young man. 'You know how things have been . . . just no time at all for—for getting married.' He spoke her own soft, fluent Spanish. 'Some day, maybe,' he added placatingly.

'You must find some nice girl,' Ynes said. A wistful note crept into her voice. 'I yearn to hold your son in my arms, as once I held you, *Stormito mio.*'

'I'm getting along all right,' grumbled Storm. 'No woman could run this house better than you. I'm comfortable enough.'

'Too comfortable,' scolded the Mexican woman. 'You have things too easy . . . not like the old señor. Ah, he was a man and he fought like a man. No time for him to get soft, what with the Apaches and cow thieves and making this big ranch for his son.' Ynes shook her head. 'The old senor would be disappointed. He was so proud of the Diamond M. You must have a son, who in turn will pass the old brand on to *his* son.'

Storm was silent, reminiscent gaze on one of the huge timbers that supported the veranda roof. His father had dragged it and its mates from the slopes of the Palos Verdes, great axe-hewn logs of yellow pine that now gleamed with the rich luster of the years.

Old Jim MacKenzie had put a hot branding iron

in his son's hands. 'You're twenty-one years old this day,' he said, 'and full partner with me in the ranch. Burn the mark deep, young feller. Some day you'll be havin' a son of your own slap the old Diamond M on this same post.'

Storm gazed soberly at the imprint made by the smoking iron. There were a lot of cattle on the range wearing that Diamond M brand.

Ynes, watching him with shrewd bright eyes, said softly, 'I heard the old señor's words to you that day.' She waggled a finger at him, added briskly, 'But to have a son, a man must first marry a wife, Stormito.'

The young boss of the Diamond M grinned, pinched out his cigarette and rose from the big manzanita chair.

'Looks like old Hendricks heading up here,' he observed. 'Wonder what brings Ben over this way from the Palos Verdes.'

'Got that girl of his with him,' Ynes said, staring at the approaching buckboard. Her tone lacked enthusiasm.

Storm MacKenzie said solemnly: 'There's an idea, Ynes. Maybe I can talk Louella into the notion of marrying me.'

'*That* one!' Outrage was in the Mexican woman's voice. 'Only over my dead body will that white trash come into this house as mistress.'

'She's right pretty,' argued the young rancher. His blue-gray eyes twinkled.

'She's no good!' declared Ynes. She flounced into the house, long full skirts fluffing like the feathers of an angry old hen.

Storm chuckled, went down the wide steps and through the garden gate into the big ranch yard. There was a careless grace to his long, lean body, and if the bronzed high-boned face was touched with a sternness beyond his years, there was good humor in his forthright look and firm mouth.

The girl in the ramshackle buckboard gave him a smile which was a curious mingling of boldness and awed shyness. She had a sulky red mouth, and dark resentful eyes.

'Hello, Louella. Long time no see you'— Storm's smile took in grandfather and daughter. 'Glad to see you, Ben. . . . Was in my mind to ride over your way. Been wanting to have a pow-wow with you.'

Hendricks shook his head gloomily. He was a gaunt, stooped-shouldered man with a melancholy unshaven face adorned with an unkempt, tobacco-stained mustache.

'Reckon it's bad news I got for you, Stormy'— Hendricks fumbled a gnawed plug of tobacco from shirt pocket and stared at it morosely. 'Been warnin' you, Stormy, been warnin' you time an' ag'in.'

Storm MacKenzie's glance went briefly to the dark, wooded slopes of the Palos Verdes. His perturbation was plain to the two watching him from

14

the buckboard. The girl broke the short silence, her voice defiant.

'I told Grandpa if he didn't do it I'd—I'd run off some place.' She choked down an angry sob. 'I— I'm just sick of livin' like a pig in a sty . . . never a cent to spend—'

'You be quiet, Louella—' Hendricks gnawed fiercely at the plug of tobacco, spat over his shoulder, and shoved the plug back into shirt pocket. 'No call for you to git noisy.'

'I want some fun—same as other girls,' whimpered Louella. 'I'm not lettin' him talk you out of it again.'

'I'm not blaming you for feeling that way, Louella,' put in Storm. His tone was gentle.

The girl's red mouth quivered. 'Anyway, if Grandpa don't sell out now to them lumber folks he maybe won't get another chance. There's been another warnin' posted on the barn. Show it to him, Grandpa . . . show him that paper we found stuck on the barn yesterday.'

Hendricks reached down into a pocket and extracted a crumpled piece of brown wrapping paper.

The young rancher's face hardened. The ugly import of those rudely scrawled words lifted his hackles.

GET OUT OR BE BURNED OUT
LAST WARNING

15

Underneath the sprawling black letters was the roughly drawn picture of a flaming torch.

'The Red Torch gang,' Hendricks said. He spoke dully. 'No sense for me to buck the Red Torchers. That's why I'm licked, Stormy. That's why I'm headed for Mesalta. I'm sellin' my place to that lumber outfit.'

'The Great Western?' Storm's eyes narrowed. 'I'm sorry, Ben. Somehow that west slope of the Verdes always seemed a part of the Diamond M. Hate like poison to see a bunch of timber wolves turn those fine trees into logs for their sawmills.'

'I'd just as soon sell out to you,' muttered Hendricks. His face reddened. 'Ain't forgettin' how your dad always hankered to own that stand o' ponderosa. Reckon that's the finest stand o' yellow pine in the territ'ry.'

'You mean you haven't closed the sale?' The relief in Storm's voice drew an angry exclamation from Louella.

'Don't you listen to him, Grandpa!' She spoke desperately. 'You promised me we'd go straight to Mesalta an' take the money Mr. Warde wrote you he'd pay.' Her mouth quivered. 'I ain't ever goin' back to the Verdes. I hate pine trees!'

The two men ignored her. 'Ain't been no money passed,' admitted Hendricks. 'Kind of hated to close the deal without no word said to you, Stormy. You always was after me for the place. Your dad never liked the way I jumped in ahead of him an'

16

got title to that timber land, but I guess it's hurt you more than it ever did him—these last years.'

'Those pine slopes just naturally belong to the Diamond M,' the young rancher said again. 'They belong to the ranch the same way my nose belongs to my face.'

'Sure am sorry, Stormy.' Hendricks wagged his head, spat over the buckboard wheel. 'I've told you how things are shapin' 'g'inst me. Here's Louella cryin' her eyes red 'cause she cain't have fun an' all like other girls, an' now the Red Torchers after me.'

'It's a trick to scare you,' Storm MacKenzie said in a hard voice. 'The Red Torchers'll never burn you out, Ben.'

'How come you figger they won't burn me out?' queried the old timber squatter.

'It's a trick,' reiterated Storm. 'You're not the first man those timber wolves have scared into selling out cheap to them.'

'Maybe I won't be burned out, but it won't stop me from bein' murdered,' Hendricks said. 'Tim Shale, over on Dutch Creek Flats, figgered he'd hold on to his timber. He begun gettin' them Red Torch warnin's to leave the High Mesa country. Tim cussed an' stomped 'round, figgered they couldn't scare him none.' Hendricks shook his head. 'Tim was found layin' there dead, crushed by a tree he was fellin'. Folks said it was an accident, but I guess me an' you know different, Stormy.

Tim Shale was murdered, same as I'll be murdered if I don't sell out.'

'I'll better the Great Western's offer, Ben. It's a bad time for me to raise money . . . means going into debt.' Storm's tone was unhappy.

'It's got to be cash money,' muttered old Hendricks, with a sidewise glance at his sulking granddaughter.

'It's got to be twenty thousand dollars'—Louella spoke with shrill vehemence—'paid cash down to Grandpa an' me by noon tomorrow.' There was no hint of awed shyness in her eyes now. They gave Storm MacKenzie a hard bright look.

Her grandfather nodded. 'That was what Warde said the lumber outfit would do,' he confirmed. 'It's plain robbery, Stormy. Four sections of the best yellow pine in Arizona. I figgered to get five times as much.'

Storm was silent for a long moment. 'Twenty thousand is a lot of cash to find inside of twenty-four hours, Ben,' he finally told the old man. 'How about a few thousand down, and the balance in yearly payments?'

'It's all or nothing,' sharply broke in Hendricks's granddaughter. She gave Storm a hard little smile that drew a surprised stare from him. There was something ruthless about this young backwoods girl. Louella was scarcely more than seventeen.

Hendricks nodded, spat again over the buck-board wheel. 'Louella's talkin' good sense,

Stormy. Up to you to give us the same deal we can get from Warde's outfit.'

'You've got me over a barrel, Ben,' grumbled the young cowman.

'She's worth the money,' declared Hendricks. 'You'll make money on the deal. Best stand o' yellow pine in the territ'ry.'

'I'm in the cattle business,' reminded Storm with a wry smile.

'Plenty good grass on them slopes,' Hendricks pointed out.

'I'm thinking about those trees. Hate to see a lumber outfit get to work on them.'

'Ruin the watershed, an' that would play hell with the ranch, Stormy. Your dad said so time an' ag'in when he'd come after me to sell out to him.'

Storm nodded. Old Hendricks spoke the truth. No matter the cost, the Palos Verdes hills had to be saved for the ranch. Water was life to the ranch, and the water came from those hills.

He came to a decision. 'You win, Ben. It's a deal. I'll meet you in Mesalta tomorrow.'

'We'll be at the hotel, Dave's place,' arranged Ben.

'Eleven o'clock,' Louella put in. 'We want that money in our hands by eleven o'clock.'

'I'll be there,' promised Storm. He looked at her curiously.

Excitement touched the girl's cheeks with quick color. She gave her grandfather a fleeting triumphant smile.

'We can go live in Phoenix . . . I can buy clothes
. . . have fun—like other girls.'

'You're goin' to school,' Hendricks told her
crustily. 'Don't you get crazy notions.' He jerked a
nod at Storm. 'See you over to Mesalta in the
mornin', Stormy.'

The buckboard rattled away, lifting clouds of
dust. Storm watched for a few moments, his
expression thoughtful. He had bound himself to a
big undertaking—and just when money was tight.
Nothing else he could have done. His father had
always said those hills meant life to the ranch.
Twenty thousand dollars was nothing compared
with the value of the watershed. Those forested
slopes had to be saved.

His gaze went to a slim Mexican youth who was
enjoying a *siesta* in the shade of a large cottonwood by the horse trough.

'Miguel!'

The Mexican came to his feet with a single,
effortless movement.

'Throw my saddle on Cacique—'

'Si, señor . . . *muy pronto*—' Miguel started on
the run toward the big barn. There was a rasp in the
boss's voice that commanded haste.

Storm made his way back to the house, again settled down in the deep manzanita chair. His father
had made that chair before Storm was born. It had
outlasted Jim MacKenzie's lifetime, and would
still be there for the grandson he had longed for.

20

From this same chair old Jim had looked across the Diamond M range to the slopes of the Palos Verdes, always regretting the procrastination that gave Ben Hendricks the opportunity to obtain title to those vast reaches of yellow pine.

Settlers in the High Mesa country were few and far between. Those timbered hills were open range. There seemed no need to acquire a more secure title. It remained for one of his own cowhands to give him the shock of his life. Jim never forgave Ben Hendricks for stealing a march on him.

Ben was from the Maine woods country, a lover of tall trees. His shrewd Yankee mind saw what Jim MacKenzie was unable to visualize. Jim was a born cowman, Ben a lumberman to the bone. One saw beauty in the majestic pine-clad heights, loved the clean fragrance of the forest and the whispered music of the wind through lofty green tops. The other man saw only board feet of lumber, and the day when the yellow pine of the Palos Verdes would mean a fortune in dollars and cents.

Once he became owner of the coveted timber, the former Diamond M cowhand took a morbid satisfaction in pride of possession. He became content to live in poverty, a miser who loved his gold too much to part with any of it. Jim MacKenzie finally gave up his efforts to buy the property from Ben.

Storm, gazing somberly at the distant wooded hills, recalled his father's prophecy. *Ben's got to come to it, some day . . . the lumber business will boom sky high . . . those fellers 'll find some way to pry Ben loose from that yellow pine. . . . When that day comes, you go the limit, son. The Palos Verdes slopes belong to the Diamond M . . . I won't be here. . . . It 'll be up to you, Stormy. . . .*

Storm MacKenzie smiled grimly. Maybe he was a fool, but he'd play the hand out, the way his father would have wanted. Raising that twenty thousand dollars meant a talk with Ed Manners. The young cowman winced. He'd no illusions about Ed Manners.

Unpleasant tingles chased up and down Storm's spine. A gamble, and no mistake, but he'd pledged his word to Ben Hendricks.

Ynes gave him a shrewd look as he came into the big kitchen.

'You are riding, Stormito—'

'Some business in Mesalta,' he told her. 'May be gone for a couple of days.'

'I heard you tell Miguel to saddle your brown horse,' Ynes said. 'There was a hardness in your voice that told me much. I am no fool, Stormito. It is because of Hendricks you make this trip to Mesalta.'

'I'm buying Ponderosa—'

'The old señor will sing in his grave.' The Mexican woman's fine eyes took on an added luster. 'It was his wish that some day the Palos Verdes would come to the Diamond M.'

22

'You don't think I'm crazy?' Affectionate amusement was in the look Storm gave her.

'You know your business,' Ynes said simply.

'*Gracias!*' Young MacKenzie bent toward her, kissed her on the cheek. '*Adios*—and your good prayers won't hurt things right now.' He swung on his heel, back into the hall, walled with logs of polished satiny yellow pine.

Ynes, watching from the kitchen doorway, saw him take down holster and gun from the rack. Her eyes clouded and with a shake of her head she turned into the kitchen. It was only lately that the young señor had returned to the old custom of carrying his gun when on ranch business. Despite her recent accusation that things were too easy for Storm, the faithful old housekeeper knew there was much to worry the boss of the Diamond M Ranch. Miguel had brought her disturbing talk of fine fat steers mysteriously missing from the range, and only the week before a Diamond M rider had been found slain in the tule swamps of the Little Mesalta.

The housekeeper's troubled gaze went to the girl stirring the contents of a big kettle with a long-handled spoon. 'Tomasa, when *El Señor* rides, tell Miguel I wish word with him.' Ynes passed on through the kitchen, her sandaled feet briskly pattering the hard-packed earthen floor. In her own room was a little shrine. She would light the candles and say a few prayers. It was a time for prayer, Ynes firmly told herself.

23

2
Mesalta—Cowtown

OLD-TIMERS in Mesalta were apt to shake their heads at any mention of the Great Western Land and Timber Company. The Little Mesalta was cattle country, long sacred to the spurred riders of the high mesa. The intrusion of the lumberjack's hobnailed boots was an indignity hard to be borne. The cow business was headed for perdition.

There were others who held more optimistic views, among them A. Solem, owner of Solem's General Merchandise Emporium, and Ed Manners, saloon proprietor, gambler, and private banker. These two prominent citizens saw boom times ahead for the little cowtown of Mesalta. They had only good words for Lester Warde, the Great Western's energetic general manager.

On the corner next to his prosperous Palace Bar, Ed Manners had erected a one-story building with a front of red Coconino sandstone and the first plate-glass window ever seen in the town. Ed sent all the way to Phoenix for a sign-painter, who did some fancy lettering in real gold leaf. Ed said it was expensive, but worth the money.

A. Solem's dark-liquid eyes took on an added brightness when he crossed over from his store for an admiring look.

```
┌─────────────────────────────────────┐
│         THE PIONEER BANK             │
│         Ed Manners, Prop.            │
│     Timber Lands     Cattle Lands    │
│              Mines                   │
└─────────────────────────────────────┘
```

Mr. Solem was deeply impressed by his fellow-townsman's up-and-comingness. He engaged the imported sign-painter on the spot to make a big sign to run the full width of the new and ornate false front that was to embellish the Emporium. The deal for the future work completed, Mr. Manners hospitably invited the Phoenix man over to the Palace Bar for a drink on the house. The unfortunate artist was a better sign-painter than he was a poker-player, and when he groggily climbed aboard the Phoenix-bound stage a few hours later, the price for his fine job of gold-leaf lettering was back in the saloon man's pockets. Ed Manners never allowed good money to get away from him. Not if he could figure out a way to prevent it.

Dave Stagg, who operated a livery-and-feed business in connection with the Stagg House, Mesalta's oldest hotel, gave Storm MacKenzie an account of the affair. 'Ed's a skunk for meanness,' Dave said with a disgusted shake of his head. He was a slow-spoken, big-framed man with an unruly shock of dark grizzled hair and a bold-featured face that he always kept scrupulously shaved. In his younger days he had been a freighter

25

and lost an eye during a brush with a raiding war party of Apaches. To conceal the disfigurement he habitually wore a black patch, which gave him a somewhat sinister look not in keeping with the truth. Dave was the soul of generosity, warm-hearted, and a loyal friend when he liked a man. He was known and highly thought of by most of the cow outfits within a hundred miles. Cowpunchers were always sure of a hearty welcome at the Stagg House, and what was more, they knew their horses were just as sure of the best care and feed at Dave Stagg's big livery barn. And Dave was never one to worry about an unpaid bill, was always ready to stake a man.

'I'll take that back,' Dave went on in his dry, deliberate voice. 'I've known skunks that was real gentlemen—put 'em 'longside Ed Manners.' His one good eye twinkled, and then, with a keen look at the young rancher, he said soberly: 'What's on your mind, Stormy? Got a kind of worried look in your eyes, like a horse that ain't sure if he's goin' to get oats—or just plain straw.'

'You're awfully close to the mark, Dave.' The Diamond M man's smile was wry. 'I'm in town for just one purpose, and I'll admit to feeling uneasy—wondering if I'll get oats—or just plain straw.'

'If it's a little cash for your payroll—' began Dave.

'Thanks, old-timer'—Storm shook his head. 'It's

26

money I'm in town for, but not for the payroll.' He told the liveryman briefly of his promise to Ben Hendricks.

The latter's expression was dubious. 'Means puttin' a plaster on your cows, Stormy, and on the ranch, too.' He shook his head. 'Don't like to see you get all tangled up in a money deal with a skinner like Ed Manners.'

'I'm not backing out now,' Storm said.

'I can savvy the way you feel about it,' Dave went on. 'Your dad always figgered the Palos Verdes should be Diamond M range . . . fretted a lot 'cause he couldn't pry them pine slopes loose from old Hendricks.' The liveryman's shaggy brows drew down in a thoughtful frown. 'If it wasn't for gettin' the money from Ed Manners the deal wouldn't be a bad one. Lumber's lookin' up, an' that ponderosa's the best yellow pine in the world.'

'There'll be no timber left when these loggers finish their dirty work,' grumbled Storm. 'They don't care a hoot what happens . . . just move on to some other place . . . leave a lot of sorry stumps behind them.'

' 'Tain't right,' agreed Dave Stagg. 'The greed o' man sure plays hell with the works o' God Almighty.'

'Ruins the watershed for the ranchers down in the valleys,' complained Storm bitterly. 'The Government should step in . . . put a stop to it.'

'Lumberin' should ought to be regerlated.' Dave stroked his chin with horny fingers. 'You could cut a sight o' timber from them Palos Verdes slopes and not hurt the stand a-tall.'

Storm repeated the comment he had made earlier to Ben Hendricks. 'I'm a cattleman,' he said curtly.

'Might as well make up your mind to it,' Dave Stagg said. 'The way beef prices is tumblin' you'll be in a doggone fix when time comes to pay off Ed Manners.'

'You're moving along a bit fast, Dave. Haven't even tackled Ed for the loan, yet.'

'I like to figger the worst that can happen,' the veteran ex-freighter said grimly. 'I was always one to look a long way ahead, figger out what I'd do if the Injuns come a-whoopin' down on my wagons.'

Storm gave him a smile in which mingled affection and deep respect. 'Well, might as well tackle Ed and have it out with him,' he said. 'See you later, Dave. I'll be staying the night at your place.'

'Sarah'll take good care of you,' assured the old man.

He left the management of the Stagg House entirely to his capable wife. Dave preferred to spend his time at his big livery barn. He liked the smell of horses and sweet hay, and enjoyed yarning with the bullwhackers and teamsters and cowboys who put up at his corrals. They kept him in touch with his old life when his huge wagons made the long haul through the Indian country to Santa Fe.

Such visitors were often the source of odd scraps of news, idle rumor for the most, but some of it important enough for Dave to tuck away for use when occasion needed.

'Just a moment, Stormy'—the old man's lowered voice swung young MacKenzie round from the office door. He sensed Dave had something on his mind. 'A feller was in from Holbrook way a night or two back, spilled a bit of news might interest you.'

Storm looked at him inquiringly. He knew Dave well enough to know that the Holbrook man's 'bit of news' concerned himself, or Dave would not waste time to pass it on.

'This feller—he was a Lazy K rider—was tellin' me that Red Yessap broke loose from the Yuma jail.'

Storm's face hardened. 'How long back?' His tone was harsh.

'Month or two back, from what this Lazy K feller said.'

Storm's eyes narrowed, and after a moment: 'Thanks, Dave. Explains a few things.'

'Figgered you should know,' Dave said. 'Red Yessap's a bad egg. He ain't one to forget 'twas you who had him put away over to Yuma.'

'I should have strung him up to the nearest tree,' Storm fretted.

'Times has changed some.' Dave's tone was tinged with regret. 'Your dad would have set Red Yessap dancin' on air.'

'Dad was a lot smarter than I am.' Storm's smile was wry. 'Going to college made me soft.'

'A man had to take the law into his own hands in your dad's day,' reminded Dave. 'It's different now, son. We've got the Law in the Territ'ry these times. We don't hold necktie parties no more, Stormy. We leave it to the Law to hang rustlers an' such.'

Storm MacKenzie nodded. He was thinking of the Diamond M rider found shot in the tule swamps of the Little Mesalta.

'Guess it explains about Wally Stevens,' he said. 'It was Wally's evidence that convicted Red Yessap.'

'Reckon you've hit the nail plumb center, Stormy. Looks like the first thing Yessap done was to lay for Wally.' Dave spoke sorrowfully. 'Sure was cut up a lot to hear about Wally Stevens. A nice young feller and a first-rate hand with cows.'

'Jim Race should know about this,' Storm worried. 'A poor time for me to be fooling around here in Mesalta—with Red Yessap on the loose.'

'Nothin' to keep you from ridin', 'cept your deal with Ben Hendricks.' The liveryman's tone was dry. 'Looks like your timber deal has got you in a doggone fix already.'

Storm glowered at him. 'It's no joke, Dave. I've

promised to have that cash for Hendricks by eleven tomorrow morning. I'm not going to let him down.'

Rain was falling in a thin drizzle as he made his way up the board sidewalk toward Ed Manners's new bank building. Absorbed in his thoughts he failed to notice the three horsemen drawing rein in front of the Palace Bar. One of the riders, a small, wiry little man with reddish hair showing under his Stetson, gave him a quick look and with a muttered word to his companions hurriedly pushed through the swing doors. The other two men craned their heads in a hard-eyed interested look at Storm, then followed the red-haired man into the saloon.

3
The Stage from Flagstaff

ED MANNERS was not in his bank. Storm crossed over to the Emporium for a look there, before trying the Palace Bar. He knew that as a rule Ed Manners seldom went to his saloon until the night was in full swing.

A. Solem popped out of his cubbyhole of an office, an affable welcoming smile on his dark full face. He was an Armenian. Like most of his countrymen he possessed a genius for business that in a few years lifted him from a peddler's wagon to the ownership of the prosperous General Merchandise Emporium. He was enormously proud of his store.

Storm shook hands. He rather liked the genial little man. What the A stood for he had no idea. The merchant was A. Solem to all who knew him.

'Ed will be over at the stage office,' he informed Storm in response to the latter's inquiry. His voice was soft, only slightly touched with the accent of his native land. 'He went over with Mr. Warde, who is expecting friends on the Flagstaff stage. Lady friends!' A. Solem rubbed his hands. 'That young Mr. Warde . . . he is a smart man. A fine thing he comes to our town, Mr. MacKenzie. He plans the biggest sawmill in the Territory. My profits already jump like this!'—A. Solem made a gesture with his expressive hands. 'A fine boom for the town, Ed Manners says.'

Storm shook his head. 'Won't be a healthy boom,' he prophesied. 'What's going to become of your boom when these timber wolves have cleaned out all the good timber and gone off leaving a lot of stumps behind for you to look at?'

'You do not like the lumber people coming here, bringing us much business?' A. Solem widened his eyes.

'I don't,' Storm said gloomily.

'What you mean?' The storekeeper pursed full red lips.

'We don't like these timber outfits horning in on us,' Storm explained. 'Cows and lumber won't mix well in the Little Mesalta country.'

'I do not understand.' A. Solem was plainly worried.

'When the loggers get through butchering the slopes it's good-bye to the watershed for a long time to come,' Storm told him. 'Leaves nothing to hold the rainfall.' He paused, added dryly, 'No grass for cows, no business for you.'

There was thought in the storekeeper's large black eyes as his gaze followed the tall cowman out to the street, then his look lifted to one of the big kerosene lamps already lighted against the early fall of darkness due to the sullen gray sky. The wick was smoking. A. Solem spoke sharply to a Mexican clerk clad in a neat blue-denim jumper.

'Where do you keep your eyes that you let my fine lamp get ruined!'

Muttering to himself, the storekeeper returned to his crowded little office. He did not like this talk from the Diamond M man. The lumber business meant boom times for Mesalta. Already the Emporium was doing twice the business. It did not matter where profits came from. Profits were profits, and he was in business to make money.

The stage from Flagstaff was rattling up the street. Storm got a glimpse of whiskered Al Penner, humped forward on the driver's seat, lines of the four-horse hitch bunched in big hands, black oilskin slicker gleaming wetly. As was his custom, Al announced his arrival with an earsplitting yell that rose above the thunder of pounding hoofs and clatter of wheels.

Storm pushed up the collar of his sheepskin coat

against the increasing drive of the rain, vaguely aware of a girl's pale face peering between the storm curtains of the stage as it swayed past him.

By the time he reached the stage office, a block down the street from the store, Al Penner was disembarking his passengers, strident voice lifted in would-be humorous pleasantries about the trip. Lester Warde was helping two ladies from the stage. The cowman recognized the younger one as the girl who had peered at him from between the storm curtains. He was conscious of warm brown eyes, a low, pleasing voice as she made some light response to the stage-driver's witticisms.

Two other passengers climbed from the coach: Burl Jenners, a cattle-buyer from Kansas City, and a short, black-overcoated man whose pair of large cases identified him as a traveling salesman. The cattle-buyer espied Storm, approached with outstretched hand.

'Hello, Stormy. Saves me a long ride, running into you like this.'

They shook hands, and Storm said hurriedly: 'See you later, Burl, over at the Stagg House. Right now I'm busy.'

Ed Manners was talking to the elder of the two women.

'Want a talk with you, soon as convenient,' Storm said to him. He gave the woman an apologetic smile. 'Awfully important, Ed.'

It was plain that Manners was puzzled by the

request. 'Make it later, say after supper, over in my office.' With a curt nod he resumed his conversation with the woman. Storm's closer view told him she was a type not often seen in the Little Mesalta country. Her smart clothes advertised her as probably from the East. She gave the young rancher a supercilious stare as he passed on.

'Yes, ma'am,' Ed Manners was suavely reassuring her in his best style, 'my Palace Hotel's the swellest house in the Southwest, bar none. Soon as Mr. Warde heard you was headin' our way he come right over and engaged the bridal soot for you.'

'Oh, Mr. Manners, how killing . . . the *bridal* suite, of all things! How amusing, *really*.' The lady tittered, threw an arch smile at the girl, who was helping Lester Warde identify their bags as Al Penner dragged them from the mud-splashed boot. 'So *amusing,* dear. Lester has engaged the bridal suite for us.'

'I don't think it's funny,' retorted the girl. She spoke crossly. 'There—that's the last of them.' She pointed out a big leather hat box. 'Come on, Mother, let's get out of this rain.' She started across the street toward the Palace Hotel. There was resentment in the way she swung her strong young shoulders.

Lester Warde's gaze followed her for a moment, a puzzled look on his big ruddy face.

'I'm afraid Fanny didn't see the joke,' laughed the mother. 'Dear Fanny is so—so literal.'

Warde, a powerful, heavy-set man in his early thirties, arrogantly handsome, said slowly: 'Perhaps it wasn't wise. Fanny is tired, and I guess she thinks all this is terribly crude.'

'She'll have to get used to it,' Fanny's mother retorted. 'Come, Mr. Manners, please help me across the street. Why didn't I bring an umbrella! And Lester, please do get our bags over at once.'

Mr. Warde was already beckoning to a couple of Mexicans lounging near the stage-office door.

Sarah Stagg greeted Storm with loud exclamations of delight. She was a big woman, with graying, rather untidy hair and pleasantly beaming face.

'Stormy, lad! 'Tis that glad I am to see your face! And how is Ynes?'

'Fine, Sarah, and that's what you're looking yourself.' His eyes twinkled.

'Go on with you!' Mrs. Stagg beamed. She cocked her head in a wise look. 'I'll be bettin' Ynes is ridin' you hard these days, lad. Ynes is mighty worried that you don't find a nice girl to put in that big ranch-house. I'm thinkin' the same, Stormy.'

For some reason, Storm was silent. All unbidden a picture had flared up in his mind, the picture of a girl with warm brown eyes—the face and fine lines of a thoroughbred. He came to himself, aware of Mrs. Stagg's curious scrutiny.

'Maybe you're right, Sarah.' His tone was sober.

'You'd a queer look in your eyes,' Mrs. Stagg said. 'I'd have sworn there was some girl in your mind just then.' She went briskly to more practical affairs. 'You can sit right down to supper, Stormy, soon as you've washed up a bit. There's an old friend of yours in the dinin'-room now, Burl Jenners. Burl hasn't been in town for a coon's age.'

The cattle-buyer looked up with a pleased smile when he saw Storm approaching his table. 'Fine,' he greeted. 'We can have a talk while we eat.' Jenners chuckled. 'Wish I was out this way more often. Mrs. Stagg sure knows her soup.'

Storm drew out a chair. 'Hello, Jenny. You're fast on the service.' He smiled at the plump carroty-haired girl who came up with a bowl of steaming soup.

'Ma Stagg said you'd be right in.' Jenny dimpled, rolled her eyes at him. 'We got strawberry shortcake tonight, Mr. MacKenzie. Ma's strawberry beds are doin' awful good this year.'

'Mr. Jenners'—Storm spoke solemnly—'you're in luck tonight. You wait until you get your nose into Ma's strawberry shortcake.'

'Won't be in no shape a-tall to sit a saddle.' Jenners's expression sobered. 'You said you couldn't see me until after supper, Stormy. Get finished with your business?'

'Manners was tied up,' Storm told him. 'Made a date to see him at his office, after supper.'

'I ain't likin' that hatchet-faced gambler too

much,' commented the cattle-buyer. 'Just as soon get tangled up with barb wire as mess round with him.'

Storm shrugged his strong shoulders. 'What's on your mind, Burl? Picking up some steers?'

'How are you fixed for a shipment, say in three months? A special deal, Stormy. I'm kind o' favorin' you for plenty good reasons, and one of 'em is you're old Jim MacKenzie's son. Jim was a square-shooter.'

'Thanks, Burl.' The young cowman's tone was laconic, but his smile was warm.

'Your Diamond M stuff is always up to grade,' Jenners went on. 'You've never let me down, Stormy, your dad nor you.' The cattle-buyer paused, looked regretfully at his empty soup bowl. 'I'm needin' one thousand prime four-year-olds,' he said briskly. 'How many can I count on from you, Stormy?'

'Four hundred, maybe a few more,' Storm told him, after a few moments' concentrated thought. 'That is, if we don't keep on losing to rustlers.'

'What do you mean, losin' to rustlers?'

'Lost close on fifty head the past month,' Storm told him gloomily. 'Looks bad, Burl. One of our boys was killed . . . found dead in the tules down in the south fork of the Little Mesalta.'

Jenners stared at him for a moment, then drew a crumpled newspaper from a pocket. 'Picked up a copy of the *Coconino Sun* in Flagstaff,' he said.

'There's an item here might interest you, Stormy.' He passed the newspaper across the table.

Storm read the paragraph in silence, then gave his friend a grim smile. 'Heard about it from Dave Stagg just before you got in on the stage, Burl,' he said. 'Dave has a way of picking up news.'

'Looks like it explains why you're losin' steers,' commented Jenners. He shook his head. 'My guess is Red Yessap has headed right back to the Little Mesalta. He's a wolf . . . a killer. He'll be gunnin' for you, raidin' your range and layin' for a chance to drygulch you.'

'I'd say you've figured things out mighty close.' Storm spoke dryly. 'I'm not scared, Burl. I nabbed Red Yessap once and I can do it again. Only this time it'll be a rope, instead of Yuma. Yessap will swing for killing Wally Stevens.'

The cattle-buyer grunted, shook his head. 'I'd hate to be in Red Yessap's boots, and *you* on my trail,' he said.

4
Trouble in the Making

ACROSS the street, a block away, Red Yessap was having a private talk with Ed Manners in the saloon office. Manners was in a disturbed frame of mind.

'I thought you were smart,' he grumbled. 'Of all the crazy notions, showin' your face in this town. You're plain loco, Red.'

The red-haired little man, sprawled in the opposite chair, looked at the saloonkeeper with slate-colored eyes. It was a curious, unwinking stare that made Ed Manners squirm uneasily. 'You've got the look of a snake about you,' he complained. 'You don't seem human, the way you fix your eyes on a feller.'

'I had to see you'—the desperado spoke in a flat, toneless voice. 'You an' me has got to stick together, Ed. No foolin'.' Yessap's lip lifted in a mirthless smile. 'I aim for you not to run out on me, if that's what you figger to do. I'm knowin' too much for you to try any double-crossin'.'

The saloon man's face took on an odd pallor and his look lowered to the open drawer of his desk.

'Don't git foolish, Ed.' The red-haired Yessap shook his head warningly. 'You leave that gun lay in the drawer. You wouldn't have a chance an' you know it.'

Ed Manners forced a laugh. 'You don't trust nobody, huh, Red?'

'Trust you less than anybody,' was the man's blunt answer. 'Don't try any tricks, Ed. I know too much about you . . . could mebbe do some talkin' 'bout this here Red Torch outfit.'

'Shut your mouth!' Manners went rigid.

'It's up to you to keep my mouth shut,' Red Yessap said with a rasping laugh. 'Keep your promises, Ed, an' you won't need to worry 'bout me.'

'If it's that money—'

'Sure it's that money!' broke in Yessap, fury in his voice. 'You promised to bring it to me—said you'd meet me at Tule Creek Fork.'

'Clean forgot,' said Manners. 'I'll have to get it from the bank safe, Red. You can wait in the bar, but don't mix 'round in there too much.'

'I can take care of myself,' grunted the outlaw. He rose from his chair, gave the other man a meaning look. 'It's seven hundred dollars, Ed. My cut for that last bunch I turned over to Vordal for you.'

Manners nodded. 'I'll bring it over to you,' he promised. 'And don't you pull off this fool play again, Red. You'll jam the works for keeps.'

The rustler's lip lifted in his mirthless smile. 'I'm givin' you a lesson,' and then: 'I seen MacKenzie when I rode in.'

Ed Manners stifled an oath, started to speak. Yessap interrupted him.

'He didn't look my way. If he had-a looked I'd have been ready'—he tapped the gun in his holster. 'I'm goin' to git him, but I'm gittin' him my own way. I want to have him alive, git some fun out of him before I kill him.' Yessap's eyes flamed. 'I'll pay him back plenty.'

'You lay off him,' Manners said angrily. 'You'll only make trouble.'

'I ain't takin' your orders,' sneered the little man. 'Play the game right and you can rustle the

Diamond M to the bone,' Manners told him. 'Use sense, Red.'

'I'll think about it,' grinned the outlaw. He pushed through the side door into the hall that led to the long barroom.

The saloon man sat for a few moments. From the look on his hard face it was apparent that his thoughts were far from pleasing. Suddenly he glanced at his watch, got out of his chair and hurriedly left the dingy office by way of the back door. Strains of dance music touched his ears as he passed down the side of the long building. His entertainers always got to work early on a Saturday night. Another hour would see the Palace Bar crowded with riders from the cow outfits and heavy-footed lumberjacks from the hills. There would be a sprinkling of cavalrymen, too, and the usual riffraff, all with money they would leave behind to fill his pockets. The thought brought a grin to the saloon man's face, somewhat eased the tension due to the troublesome Red Yessap. He'd find a way to deal with Yessap, but he'd have to go slowly. Red was speaking the truth when he said he knew too much.

Storm MacKenzie was crossing the street from the Stagg House when Manners reached the plate-glass front of his new bank building.

'Hello, Ed'—Storm put a match to his cigarette. 'No need to go into your office. . . . Just want to ask you a question.'

'What's on your mind?' Manners drew a cigar from a pocket, bit off the end. He was puzzled by the young cowman's plainly embarrassed manner.

'I need some cash . . . quite a hunk.'

'Guess we can fix you up,' Manners told him affably. 'That's what I got this bank for, makin' loans to good customers.'

'I want twenty thousand—for ninety days.'

'That's a lot of money,' observed the banker. 'What security?'

'My note.'

Manners frowned. 'You're crazy.'

Storm was silent for a moment. He had originally intended to ask for a three-year loan, with ranch and cattle as security. His talk with Burl Jenners had changed his plan. The price offered by the cattle-buyer for four hundred and fifty prime four-year-olds would be more than sufficient to take care of the loan. Delivery was to be in ninety days, in time to get the cash to take up the note.

He explained the situation to Manners. He had the steers, and Jenners was not the man to go back on a deal.

'What do you want the money for?' Manners's tone was wary. 'It's a banker's right to know, MacKenzie.'

'I'm buying Ponderosa from old Ben Hendricks.' Storm made the statement with some reluctance. He hated being forced to give the details.

Ed Manners stared at him curiously. 'The Palos

Verdes, huh!' He drew hard on his cigar. 'I don't know what to say right now, MacKenzie. Guess I'll have to think it over.'

'I've got to know *now.*'

Manners's poker face gave no hint of the thoughts boiling in his scheming mind. It was too good to be true, but he'd have to have a talk with Lester Warde before he could make a deal with Storm MacKenzie.

'I'll tell you in the morning,' he said. 'Got to think it over, but I've an idea we can fix it up for you, MacKenzie.'

'I'm depending on it.'

'I guess you can count on me,' Manners reassured him. 'It's a big loan. You can't blame me for wantin' to think it over.'

Storm went back to the Stagg House and up to his room. He lit the coal-oil lamp and sank into a chair. Something brushed against his hand as he fumbled in a pocket for his pipe—Jenners's copy of the *Coconino Sun.* He drew the little newspaper out, scanned the columns idly, his mind going over his talk with Ed Manners. Suddenly he straightened in his chair, his interest caught by a small paragraph.

FAIR VISITORS FROM THE EAST
Mrs. Horace Winston and her daughter, Miss Fanny, arrived today in Flagstaff, en route to Mesalta, where they plan an extended visit

with Mr. Lester Warde, the Great Western Timber and Land Company's genial General Manager. It is whispered that Romance with a capital R brings Miss Winston to Mesalta. The Sun wishes Mr. Warde the best of luck. . . .

Storm's face darkened. For some reason he found the paragraph vaguely disturbing. He re-read the thing with increasing annoyance. This Fanny Winston was the girl he had seen standing in the rain in front of the stage office. Again he saw that pale face peering at him through the storm curtains of the stage rocking past. Something had reached out from her, a wistful appeal that had sent an odd thrill through him. She had seemed competent enough those few moments later at the stage office, quietly poised, and singularly oblivious of Lester Warde's posses-sive manner.

Storm found his already fervent dislike of the Great Western's general manager growing. He threw the newspaper to the floor, the growl of a bristling dog in his throat. He could not join with the *Coconino Sun* in wishing Lester Warde the best of luck.

5
The Crash of Guns

THE same item of news in the Flagstaff *Coconino Sun* that so curiously disconcerted Storm MacKenzie was the subject of a heated discussion between the two ladies occupying the bridal suite of the Palace Hotel.

'It's hateful,' Fanny Winston told her mother. 'Anybody would think I'm engaged to marry Lester.'

Mrs. Horace Winston's eyebrows arched in a quizzical look at her daughter. 'Well—isn't becoming engaged the one and only reason why we have come all the way from New York to this barbarous western country? Lester thinks so.'

'The country is all right,' Fanny declared. 'I like it, only I—I don't like Lester very much, Mother. I—I wish you hadn't made me come.' She went to the window, stood there, staring down into the street. Blue sky had replaced the sullen gray clouds of the previous night, and the breeze coming through the open window had a winelike tang to it. An Indian rode past on an ambling pinto pony. A red headband adorned his long black hair. He wore a gaily colored blanket, and buckskin pants ornamented with large silver buttons. Behind him on another pony rode a squaw, her neck and arms loaded with silver and turquoise jewelry. Navajos, the girl guessed. The sight of them thrilled her, chased the mutinous look from her eyes. After all, there were compensations. Fanny knew that she was already completely in love with Arizona, if not with the man she had come to marry. Lester Warde wanted the marriage, but she had never been able to face it.

Mrs. Winston was watching her daughter with shrewd but not unkindly eyes. Fanny would live to thank her for getting her married off to so splendid a catch as Lester Warde. Even if Lester's venture in these wild timberlands failed, there would still be the paternal Warde millions. But Lester would not fail. The Wardes had the magic touch that turned things to gold.

She broke the silence. 'I think it is time we went down and saw about some breakfast, dear.'

The girl smiled round at her. 'It's a glorious day. I can scarcely wait to get outdoors.' She stretched out her arms, drew in deep breaths of the tangy air. 'I'm already in love with this Arizona.'

Mrs. Winston repressed a shudder. She felt it was discreet not to express her own unflattering opinions of Arizona. If things went as she fervently hoped they would, Arizona was to be her daughter's home. Mrs. Winston realized that Fanny's liking for the dreadful place was just so much resistance overcome.

'Not much like New York'—the mother's smile was indulgent—'but most picturesque, and—and extremely exciting. I—I really envy you, Fanny, such a wild, free land for your home.' Mrs. Winston's regretful sigh was very well done. 'But of course, it must be New York again for me, once you are safely married. Lester wouldn't want a fussy old mother-in-law around the place.'

There was no smile on the girl's face as she looked at her mother. She knew what was in the older woman's mind. Lester would be paying her mother's bills. It would be part of the bargain. The daughter—sold to the highest bidder. Fanny knew it, but was helpless. They were practically penniless and there seemed no other way out.

'I'm starving for breakfast,' Mrs. Winston said plaintively.

Fanny forced a smile. 'Lester promised he'd have breakfast with us,' she reminded brightly. 'Lester is really very sweet to us.'

Mrs. Winston went downstairs in a state bordering on exaltation. Fanny was giving in at last. It seemed a miracle too good to be true. A sharp glance at the girl reassured her. No hint of a cloud in those fine, frank eyes, so like her dead father's. Fanny was the image of her father in all ways.

Lester Warde met them in the hotel lobby and asked to be excused from taking breakfast with them. There was an urgent business call, he explained, but he would meet them later and take them on a drive and show them the site for the new big sawmill.

He hurried away, looking back from the door to send a smile to the girl. She waved a hand for her mother's benefit, was rewarded by a beatific look.

'Lester is so fine and masterful,' purred Mrs. Winston. 'Really, dear, he is a very thrilling young man.'

Fanny pretended to be interested in the approaching Mexican waitress. She could go just so far, but not far enough to agree that she saw anything to thrill her in Lester Warde.

The latter found Ed Manners waiting for him in the new bank office, seated at the big desk recently imported from Phoenix. Ed was enormously proud of his desk.

'Real oak,' he informed young Warde; 'cost me all of a hundred, not countin' the freight.'

'What's on your mind, Ed?' queried the lumberman. 'You didn't call me over to show me your new desk, did you?'

Manners frowned at the long ash on the end of his cigar. He had a thin-lipped, lean face scored with harsh lines, and sandy, receding hair. He might have been in his late forties or early fifties, tough and wiry and wary-eyed.

'Got some news you won't like,' he said. 'Old Hendricks is sellin' his Palos Verdes place to Storm MacKenzie.'

Lester Warde's big blond face darkened.

'Makes you kind of hit the ceiling, huh?' Ed

Manners's lips creased in what he thought was a smile.

'I was to have the first chance, when that gang of yours got him scared into selling,' fumed the lumberman. 'Looks like you've bungled things.'

'The scheme worked good with Tim Shale,' reminded Manners with another grin. 'You got hold of Tim's Dutch Flats timber, didn't you—an' at your own figure.'

'Old Shale hadn't much to say about it.' Warde's tone was uneasy. 'I made the deal with his heirs.' The lumberman frowned. 'I wouldn't talk too much about Tim Shale. Some of the people in this town don't feel satisfied with the coroner's verdict on that case.'

'Who's talkin'?'

'Dave Stagg, for one, and I guess he's repeating only what he hears. Dave picks up a lot of news, and he's smart.'

'Mebbe too smart for his own good,' sneered Manners. He flung his cigar into a large brass cuspidor by the side of his desk and straightened up in the swivel chair. 'I'm not goin' to let that old mule-skinner get too smart with me . . . upset my plans.'

'Dave Stagg is popular with the cowmen,' Warde pointed out. 'I'd advise you to watch your step with *him*.'

'You an' me can run things in this Little Mesalta country if we don't get cold feet,' Manners said softly. 'You leave fellers like Dave Stagg an' Storm MacKenzie to me.'

Warde's eyes widened in a look of inquiry. 'MacKenzie?' His tone was sharp.

'MacKenzie hasn't paid old Hendricks his money—yet,' Manners told him.

The lumberman's face brightened. 'Then there's still time to beat him to it, only we've got to work fast.'

Ed Manners shook his head. 'Too late to head off the deal now, Les'—He ignored the younger man's half-frown at the familiar use of his name. 'Old Hendricks is a shiftless sort of cuss, but he ain't one to go back on his word. He's due in town today, to get his money from MacKenzie, twenty thousand dollars, same as you was fixin' to pay him for that Ponderosa place.'

'I'd like to wring the old man's scrawny neck,' muttered Warde. 'I've got to have that stand of yellow pine. Puts a crimp in things.'

'I got a scheme that'll maybe work out good for both of us,' Manners said with a leer. 'Old Hendricks is due in town for his money, but MacKenzie ain't got the twenty thousand cash ready.'

Warde frowned. 'What's the idea, scaring me to death when you knew MacKenzie couldn't go through with the deal?'

'He wants to borrow the money from me.' Manners grinned. 'I figger to let him have the money, Les.'

'You're crazy!' Warde's tone was incredulous. 'I don't get you, Ed.'

'MacKenzie figgers to give me his note, claims he can pay it off in ninety days. I figger he's wrong. That's why it'll be a good deal to loan him the twenty thousand.'

Warde shook his head. 'I know you've got the brains of a fox, Ed, but I can't follow your reasoning. All I know is that MacKenzie gets that stand of yellow pine away from me.'

'MacKenzie don't want to give me any security for the note,' Manners continued. 'He's in a box, though, an' he won't balk when I tell him he's got to give me a lien on that Ponderosa place as security. I'll fix the paper to read that if the note ain't paid on the day she's due he's got to sign me a quitclaim deed to them Palos Verdes hills.'

'I still don't see the point,' grumbled Warde.

'I was just tellin' you that MacKenzie won't be in shape to pay off the note when she's due.' Sly amusement lurked in the saloon man's narrow-slitted eyes. 'That's why I want you to put up the twenty thousand dollars, Les.'

'For *him?*' Warde stuttered angrily. 'You're crazy, Ed, if you think I'm going to lend you twenty thousand dollars to lend to MacKenzie to buy that yellow pine I want.'

'Not so crazy,' protested Manners. 'I turn that note over to you an' ninety days from now you'll be owner of them Palos Verdes slopes. It's a sure bet, Les.'

The lumberman stared at him for a long moment. Something he read in the other man's shrewd eyes seemed to reassure him.

'Supposing MacKenzie *does* pay the note?' His tone was cautious, thoughtful.

'He won't.' Manners spoke softly. 'I'll see to it that MacKenzie won't pay that note, Les.' He glanced at his watch. 'How about it? Do I get that twenty thousand?'

Warde pondered. 'Where do you come in?' he wanted to know. 'Don't see any profit for you, in the deal.'

'I'll take care of myself,' smiled Manners. His face hardened. 'I'll get plenty profit by the time I'm finished with that spur-jinglin' cowman.'

Warde seemed satisfied. He nodded. 'It's a deal, Ed. I'll get the money from my office safe. Had it waiting for Hendricks to show up.'

'I'll go see MacKenzie—' Manners broke off, looked at his plate-glass window. 'He's crossin' the street now, headed this way. Guess he's gettin' nervous. Told him last night I wasn't sure I'd make the loan.'

Storm met Warde at the door as the lumberman left the office. They exchanged curt nods. Storm knew he had no real reason to dislike the big blond man, but he did. Warde was an interloper, a menace to the country that had long been cattle range. Also the sight of him recalled the paragraph in the *Coconino Sun.*

Manners jerked a nod at the departing Warde. 'Been tellin' him about your deal with Hendricks,' he said as Storm dropped into a chair. 'He's fit to be tied, losin' that yellow pine. Was all set to close with Hendricks.'

'How about that loan?' Storm spoke curtly.

Manners reached into a pocket and drew out a fresh cigar. 'Ain't makin' it, MacKenzie—not without some good security.'

'I'm not placing a mortgage on the Diamond M,' Storm said flatly.

'Ain't askin' for it,' rejoined Manners. 'Just figger for you to give me a lien on the Ponderosa place. Guess it ain't more'n fair, MacKenzie.'

The solution had not occurred to Storm. It eliminated any chance of putting the ranch in jeopardy. He wanted the money to buy the Palos Verdes. As Manners said, it was only fair to put up the newly purchased property as security for the cash he wanted to borrow.

'Shouldn't worry you none,' Manners pointed out. 'You was sayin' you'll have the money from your steers in plenty time to pay the note. An' if you don't pay the note when she's due you stand to lose only the property you're borrowin' the money to give Hendricks for.'

'Seems fair enough,' admitted Storm. 'Hadn't worked the thing out, Ed. All right, it's a deal.'

Manners nodded, got out of his chair and went to his big safe.

'Here's the cash.' He returned with a thick roll of banknotes. 'Sign that paper I've fixed up, young feller. Guess it covers the deal all right.'

Storm read the single sheet carefully. Nothing wrong about it, merely stipulated that he give Manners a quitclaim deed for the property in case of default. He took the pen from Manners's fingers and hurriedly wrote in his signature.

'Guess that settles it,' observed Manners. 'Now you can pay old Hendricks like you promised.'

'Mighty obliged to you, Ed.' Storm was really grateful, vastly relieved.

Manners went to the window, watched him cross the street and make for the Stagg House down the block. The saloon man's face wore a satisfied look. Whistling tunelessly, he went back to his desk and picked up the signed note. His smile widened, and carefully placing the paper inside an envelope, he carried it to the safe.

Ben Hendricks and Louella were in the lobby of the Stagg House.

'He's comin' now, Grandpa,' the girl said excitedly. She looked at the old clock above the lobby desk. 'It's 'most eleven, but I guess he's got the money. He's just come out of the bank.'

'Wasn't worryin',' commented Hendricks.

'Stormy's like his pa. Jim MacKenzie never went back on his word.'

'I'll bet Mr. Warde would have given us more than twenty thousand dollars,' Louella said discontentedly. 'We should have had him an' Stormy workin' against each other.'

'You talk like a little crook,' grumbled her grandfather. 'Ain't carin' for it, Louella. 'Tain't seemly in a young girl like you.'

Her sullen red mouth tightened mutinously. 'I like money and I don't care how I get it. An' Grandpa, soon as we get our money we're movin' over to the Palace for as long as we stay in Mesalta. I'm goin' to have things different from this old Stagg House dump.'

Ben looked at her with bewildered eyes. Louella was growing up fast . . . she was getting too much for him.

Storm's expression as he clattered into the lobby told them all was well. Ben extracted a neatly folded paper from a pocket.

'Reckon this makes Ponderosa yours, Stormy, soon as you've paid over the money. Went an' had Ron Petersen make out the deed quick as Louella an' me got into town. Ron's a notary an' swore to my signature. Made Louella sign, too.'

Storm handed the roll of banknotes over to the old man. 'Here's the twenty thousand, Ben.'

Louella snatched the money from him greedily. 'I'm countin' it,' she said.

'Reckon if Stormy says there's twenty thousand dollars in that roll you don't need to count it over,' chided her grandfather.

'It's my money as much as yours,' pouted the girl. She riffled through the notes, lips moving in an inaudible tally.

Storm refrained from advising Ben to put the money in some safe place. Louella would see to that.

'Well, Stormy'—Hendricks gave the cowman a toothless smile—'Cain't help but think it's right for Ponderosa to come into Diamond M range. Guess I played your pa a mean trick when I jumped in ahead of him like I did.' He scowled. 'Louella 'lows 'twas you that put the Red Torchers up to scarin' us into sellin' the place. I tell her she's pure loony.'

'You haven't much use for me, Louella.' Storm looked at the girl with amused eyes.

'Not much.' Her head lifted in a swift glance. 'Not any more'n you have for me.' Her look lowered to the fat roll of banknotes in her lap. 'You wait till I spend some of this money on clothes—an' things. You'll think I'm worth lookin' at.'

'You're a queer kid.' His tone was gentle, a bit troubled.

'I'm a woman!' she said fiercely. 'You wait, Mister Stormy MacKenzie. I'll show you!'

The bewildered look was back in Ben's eyes as he stared at his granddaughter. 'I cain't make you out, Louella. You shouldn't be talkin' like that to Stormy. 'Tain't right.'

'I'll say one thing to Louella'—the cowman's voice was crisp—'I've nothing to do with the Red Torchers.'

'You've always wanted Ponderosa for cattle range,' the girl said. 'You were mad because Grandpa wouldn't sell it to you.'

'I don't want Ponderosa for range. The Diamond M has plenty of range.' Storm gave the girl an exasperated look. 'It wasn't any cowman who got Tim Shale's place. The Red Torchers were after him, too.'

'There's talk that Tim's son, over in Tucson, has sold out to the Great Western,' Ben broke in.

Storm stared at him questioningly, and Ben hurriedly added, 'I ain't meanin' the Great Western's mixed up any with the Red Torchers.'

'I'm sure I don't care who the Red Torchers are,' Louella declared. Her lips parted in a contented smile. 'They done a good thing for me when they scared you into sellin' Ponderosa, Grandpa.'

Storm went off, inwardly fuming, yet conscious of a feeling of sympathy for the strange girl. She'd had a hard, lean time of it.

Burl Jenners was standing in front of the stage office, talking to Pete Kendall, owner of the Lazy K outfit.

The Holbrook cowman, short, stocky, and with a

somewhat belligerent red face, waved a beckoning hand.

'Guess you've heard the news about Red Yessap breakin' loose from jail,' he said as Storm came up.

'Dave was telling me,' admitted Storm. 'Got the news from one of your boys.'

Kendall nodded, shook his head worriedly. 'Keep your eyes open, Stormy. This Yessap hombre is after your scalp.'

'Thanks, Pete.' Storm looked at the cattle-buyer. 'I'll be cuttin' out those steers for you, Burl. . . . Get them in good shape for the drive.' He moved on down the board walk, his long, easy stride perceptibly slowing as he reached the Palace Hotel. The Winston girl was standing there, talking to a young Navajo woman. The Indian woman looked up as Storm approached, gave him a timid little smile of recognition.

'Hello, Maria!' The cowman halted. He remembered her well, the wife of a Navajo who ran a flock of sheep near the Painted Desert country. 'How is John Joseph?'

'He very good, señor—' the woman spoke in halting mission-school Spanish. 'This lady—' Maria gestured at the girl—'she want to buy from me.' The comely Navajo touched a silver-and-turquoise bracelet on her slender brown wrist. 'We cannot talk good.'

Storm looked at the American girl, met her smile. 'Maria says you want to buy her bracelet.'

'Perhaps I'm dreadfully rude.' Fanny spoke apologetically. 'I was told these Indians were always eager to sell such things.'

Fanny was suddenly a little breathless. This was the man she had noticed when she peered through the storm curtains of the stage. The moment was still oddly alive with her. He seemed so quietly competent, so completely in command of himself with his forthright look and easy grace of tall strong body. That fleeting interchange of looks as the stage rocked up the street had curiously affected her. Fanny wondered if he would remember. His next words told her he did.

'I saw you on the stage last evening. Rather a damp welcome to Mesalta.'

'Today makes up for it,' Fanny declared. 'There's nothing so blue as this Arizona sky.' Her smile went to the young Navajo woman. 'I suppose she makes these things herself. I'm told the Navajos do wonderful work with silver.'

Storm shook his head. 'No, Maria didn't make her bracelets. The men do the work in silver. Weaving is what the Navajo women do—rugs, and things.' He changed to Spanish. 'The lady likes your bracelet very much, Maria. Will you sell it, as a favor to me?'

'*Si*, it is hers, señor, but not for money.' The Navajo slipped the silver-and-turquoise ornament from her wrist and held it out to Fanny. 'It is because you are a good friend to John Joseph and me,' Maria added, smiling shyly at Storm.

The latter shook his head as Fanny began fumbling in her purse. 'Please don't. She would be offended.'

'Oh, but I can't!' Fanny was embarrassed.

'Some little gift in return,' smiled Storm. 'Maria has a year-old baby girl.' He nodded at the store across the street. 'Some little thing the baby can wear.'

'I'd love to do that,' Fanny said. She clasped the bracelet around her wrist, smiled her thanks at Maria.

'It would make the lady very happy to send a little gift to your baby,' Storm told the Navajo in Spanish. 'You will go with her over to the store, no?'

'*Si.*' Maria beamed, nodded pleased acquiescence.

'Thank you so much for helping us—' Fanny hesitated, an inquiring look in her eyes.

'I'm Storm MacKenzie,' the young cowman told her simply.

'And I'm Fanny Winston,' smiled the girl. She turned to follow Maria across the street to the Emporium.

Three horsemen swung out of the alley from the rear of the Palace Bar. Dust drifted in their wake. Fanny stopped to let the riders go by. One of them was a red-haired man wearing leather chaps and a wide-brimmed hat. A gun was suddenly in his hand, smoke and flame belched from the black muzzle.

The shocked girl looked over her shoulder, saw Storm MacKenzie standing where she had left him. A gun was in his hand.

The gunshots stunned her ears. All three of the riders were shooting now at the tall man on the sidewalk.

It was over in a moment, two of the horsemen spurring furiously down the street. A riderless buckskin trailed them at a gallop. Only the acrid smell of gun smoke, a momentary hush, and dust clouds that lifted to reveal the body of a man lying in the middle of the street.

Fanny stared with horrified eyes. Her ears ached from that blasting crash of gunfire. Suddenly the stillness was broken by a clamor of excited voices. Men seemed to appear magically from nowhere.

The girl saw Storm MacKenzie coming toward her. She had never seen a face so cold, so completely devoid of emotions. His eyes were like blue ice. They frightened her.

He passed her without so much as a glance, bent over the dead man lying in the dust. Fanny heard his voice, hard, bitter. He was speaking to a man who had come running from the livery barn. The man wore a black patch over one eye.

'Looks like my shooting is not so good, Dave. My bullet missed Red Yessap a mile. Got this man instead.'

His callousness revolted the girl. Revulsion made her feel sick. She longed desperately to get back to her room in the hotel, but the Indian woman was waiting for her in the store, and she had promised a little gift.

Fanny Winston's legs seemed like rubber under her as she went on across the street. She felt that she never wanted to see Storm MacKenzie again.

6
Rustlers on the Rimrock

THE herd moved slowly between low brush-covered ridges that pushed fanwise into the mesa from high red cliffs. Jim Race, riding point, swung his horse up a sloping bank and drew rein. His keen, sun-wrinkled eyes sharply scrutinized the bawling procession as it drifted past.

The Diamond M foreman's craggy, weathered face wore a contented look. He was perhaps in his middle fifties, an experienced and wise cowman.

The several hundred cattle that now crowded the narrowing funnel-like entrance into Red Canyon represented a week's combing of the cedar brakes east of Little Mesalta Creek. It had been grueling work, rounding up those strays out of the countless ravines and potholes. Wild as any deer, this bunch of nondescript baldfaces, which was why Jim had decided to bring them to Red Canyon Corral. Easier to hold them there while the likely steers were sorted out and the hot iron used on the unbranded young stock.

The foreman made a mental tally as the clamorous herd surged past. At least fifty steers, three- and four-year-old stuff. A bit gaunt, but he'd push them up the canyon to Wild Horse Flats. Good grass up there. A few weeks would have them in first-rate condition for the market. The others would be allowed to find their way back to the cedar brakes they loved. Most of them were cows with calves, with a sprinkling of surly old bulls and yearling steers.

Three men rode up with the last of the stragglers. Jim Race pushed down the bank and joined them. One of the riders turned a dust-begrimed face.

'Reckon the worst's done over with, Jim, an' I'm shoutin' loud I ain't weepin' a-tall to see these dog-gone dogies rompin' into Red Canyon Corral.'

'Don't blame you none, Jericho,' the foreman chuckled.

'Worse'n lookin' for needles in a strawpile,' grumbled Jericho. He was a merry-eyed youngster with sandy hair and a week's growth of yellow fluff on his pleasant, sunburned face. 'Trouble with these cedar-brakes cows is they ain't never been to school. No manners a-tall. Chouse 'em out of one pothole an' they head straight for the pot-hole next door. Just won't stay put no place.'

'We'll teach 'em some manners when we git 'em in Red Canyon Corral,' observed a lanky, lugubrious-faced man who wore an enormous Mexican sombrero known as a steeple hat. He was down on the Diamond M payroll as Andrew Hawkins, but nobody thought of calling him anything but High Hat. For all his long sad face he was popular with the outfit because of an unfailing even temper and dry humor.

They rode through the gap, between towering red cliffs, horses' hoofs rattling on the stones of a small dry wash. Jim Race's reason for bringing the wild cedar-brakes cattle to the canyon was quickly apparent. The place was a natural amphitheatre, walled by tier upon tier of giant upright slabs of red rock. A second gap, leading into the main fork of the canyon, was barred with a stout pole fence. No chance for the most agile steer to escape, once the bars were put in place across the lower gap. The Diamond M had worked cattle in Red Canyon Corral, as it was called, for years.

A small spring of water flowed from a crevice in the upper wall, ran in a clear shallow stream over a rock bed until it sank from sight in the dry wash. The leg-weary cattle began to drink immediately.

Jim Race watched them thoughtfully. He was remembering something Storm MacKenzie had said. The foreman's look shifted to the swarthy-faced cowboy who had ridden over to inspect the fence across the upper gap. 'Sooner, reckon you're elected to put in the first hitch watchin' things here. The boss figgers we got to be some careful—now Red Yessap's on the loose ag'in.'

'Sure,' grunted the cowboy. 'Just as soon stay now as later.'

'Keep your eyes peeled,' counseled the foreman.

'Ain't forgettin' Wally Stevens.' Sooner Bass swung from his saddle, fumbled cigarette papers and tobacco sack from shirt pocket. 'You tell Barbecue he's gotta save out plenty steak for me. I'd sooner eat poison than eat any more o' that baa-baa stew.'

Jim Race allowed a smile to crease his face. 'Barbecue's still got a couple more of them sheep left, Sooner. I'll tell him to go kind o' slow on 'em . . . save 'em for Sunday dinners.'

'I'd sooner fill my stummick with poison,' declared Sooner. 'I'm a cowman . . . gotta have my good red meat.'

'You're sure oncivilized, Sooner,' chided High Hat. 'Sheep meat is awful polite food. You gotta learn your stummick to mind its manners.'

'I'm bettin' they was old goats that Basque sheep feller give Barbecue for lettin' him make camp down on the creek that night.' Sooner's tone was disgusted.

He let down the fence bars, stood watching until the other men vanished from view. It would be long after dark before he would be relieved from guard duty. Sooner snubbed his cigarette butt against a rock, produced a lone sandwich from saddlebag, and made himself comfortable on a flat boulder by the side of the little spring. The cowboy little suspected that he was closely watched by two pairs of eyes.

The owners of the eyes were crouched high above him, on the rimrock. They were well concealed in that maze of tumbled red boulders.

One of the men reached a hand to the rifle lying by his side. 'Easy shot from here,' he muttered. 'Cain't miss him.'

His red-headed companion shook his head. 'You ain't got good sense, Vordal.'

'He's a Diamond M feller,' grumbled Vordal. 'What's got in your craw, Red? It's a cinch to git him. All o' four hundred head o' cows down there, an' the road clear to head 'em for Tule Creek Fork.'

'I'm playin' for bigger game,' Red Yessap retorted. 'I've been figgerin' MacKenzie's play. He aims to gather that bunch o' steers an' hold 'em up in Wild Horse Flats. Good grass up on them flats— keep the steers in shape when time comes for the drive.' Red Yessap licked thin lips. 'We'll all of us be up here on the rimrock when that day comes, Vordal. There'll be close on five hundred head o' fat steers down there in that stone corral. MacKenzie'll be there, too, an' all his outfit.'

'I git you, Red.' The black-bearded man's eyes glowed with the red light of a killer.

'Easy as pot-shootin' rabbits. Won't be no Diamond M outfit left to tell what went on here.' The outlaw's smile widened.

'MacKenzie got the Gila Kid that day you was in Mesalta,' Vordal reminded him softly.

Red Yessap let loose a torrent of blasphemous words. 'MacKenzie's my meat,' he told his companion. 'That's orders, Vordal. I'm gettin' MacKenzie.'

The two men cautiously made their way to a clump of scraggly piñons. A third man waited there with the horses. He gave Red Yessap an inquiring look. The latter shook his head.

'MacKenzie wasn't down there in the stone corral, Tonto.'

Tonto looked at his hand, wrapped in a soiled bandage. 'I'd sure like to git that hombre.'

'We'll pay him off good,' promised Yessap.

'The Kid was my best friend,' Tonto said with an oath.

'We'll pay him for the Gila Kid, too.' The outlaw chief turned to his horse. 'Let's ride, fellers. We got things here spotted first rate an' I want to wise up Ed Manners to the deal. Ed said he'd be waitin' at the old place down in the South Fork.'

7
A Meeting in the South Fork

THE problem of Lester Warde was not getting any easier for Fanny Winston. The more she saw of Lester the less she liked him. He was begging her to name the day for a marriage that every moment was becoming more repugnant to her. She felt hopelessly trapped.

The girl pulled her horse to a halt on the brink of the rimrock, stared miserably at the amazing panorama spread below. It was a scene that no one could look at for long and not feel an odd stirring of the heart; and as the majesty of the view filled her eyes Fanny found it impossible to cling to troublesome thoughts. They seemed too petty in the face of this mad, preposterous scenery. The color almost made her eyes ache, giant slabs of red rock standing on end, and vast buttes that seemed to lift above the distant shimmering pink sea that she knew was the Painted Desert.

A mad place, this Arizona country, weirdly and savagely beautiful. Weird people, too, some of them. Men who could ruthlessly kill their fellow-creatures. Men like Storm MacKenzie.

Fanny's face clouded. That terrible affair was remaining too vividly with her. She wanted to put it out of her mind—put Storm MacKenzie out of her mind.

He had not spoken to her again. She had remained in A. Solem's store until sure he was gone. Some men had come and carried the victim of his bullet away. It was all too dreadful. Fanny wanted desperately to forget it, forget Storm MacKenzie. But she couldn't forget Storm MacKenzie. His face came back to her at the oddest moments, sometimes as he had looked when talking to her and the Indian woman. He had seemed so fine, his face a bit stern, but kindly. And then she would see him as he looked when crossing the street toward the slain man . . . the terrible deadliness of him—the frightening ice-blue eyes.

The girl shook her head impatiently. The man was nothing to her . . . never would or could be. She was an idiot, allowing herself to think of him. She swung the horse back to the down trail.

The slopes of the big canyon were covered with scrubby-looking piñon trees. A deer, followed by a fawn, broke across the trail. Fanny reined the horse to a standstill, watched them vanish with light springy bounds.

The trail was steep in places, sometimes nothing less than miniature rocky precipices washed out by summer cloudbursts. The horse seemed sure-footed, and very wise. Fanny had hired him from the man at the big livery barn. Another weird person, Dave Stagg, with the black patch over his eye and dry, drawling voice. Fanny liked the old man. Ed Manners made fun of him, called him the old mule-skinner and other queer names like mossyhorn bullwhacker. She sensed that Dave Stagg hadn't much use for Ed Manners. Fanny didn't like the banker either. He was worse than weird. He was plain odious, always smirking and trying to be gallant to her mother. Fanny couldn't abide him. She wished her mother were less friendly with the man. Mrs. Winston was only in her late forties and still an attractive woman. Fanny had uneasy moments about her and Ed Manners. According to Lester Warde the man was rich, sole owner of his bank and the Palace Hotel. Her mother's greediness for money was too shocking. She didn't seem to mind the fact that Mr. Manners also owned a saloon, that his real business was running a saloon and dance hall.

It came to the girl with something of a shock that she must get her mother away from Mesalta and safely back in New York, before she did something dreadful—like marrying a saloonkeeper. Again, all unbidden, she saw the grave young face of Storm MacKenzie, recalled the impact of his steady, resolute eyes as she passed him in the stagecoach. She frowned, shook her head, gave her thoughts to the widening canyon.

She knew she was in the south fork of Red Canyon. Old Dave Stagg had recommended the view from the rimrock. A mile or two farther down would bring her to Tule Creek, close to the trail that cut across the mesa toward town.

Fanny glanced apprehensively at the bit of blue sky showing above the canyon walls. She would have to hurry to reach town before dark.

Suddenly she was noticing her horse. The gray's head was up, ears pricked forward. Fanny tightened the reins, came to a halt. The horse heard something missed by her less acute ears. Presently she caught a sound. Horses' hoofs, somewhere up in the small gorge that twisted down to the canyon floor. There was no time for her to ride on past the mouth of the gorge. She would run into the unseen horsemen.

She looked about desperately for a hiding place, espied two great masses of slab rock two or three times taller than herself. She climbed from her saddle, led the horse into the V-shaped niche, and tied the animal to a tough-looking shrub. It was a dark, cavelike place. Summoning her courage the girl crawled to the small crack where the two boulders came together and peered through.

Three men were riding out of the narrow gorge. They were coming in her direction. She watched fearfully, saw them halt their horses some twenty yards away. The man in the lead climbed from his saddle, stood there, staring around suspiciously. His voice faintly touched the girl's ears.

'Was sure I heard somethin' down here when we come out of the gully. Figgered it was Ed.'

'Must have been rocks tumblin' from the cliffs,' suggested one of his companions, a black-bearded man. 'Rocks is always slidin' down these canyon walls.'

'Could have sworn it was a horse,' argued the first speaker. 'Reckon you're right at that, Vordal. Must have been rocks I heard.'

Fanny's eyes widened as she peered at him through the little opening in the slabs. That light reddish hair under the wide-brimmed hat, the cruel thin-lipped mouth and bright restless eyes. She had seen him before, in Mesalta, riding down the street, smoke and flame pouring from the gun in his hand. Her heart turned over. Red Yessap! The recognition hit her like a blow in the face. Storm MacKenzie's brief utterance came back to her . . . *missed Red Yessap a mile. . . .*

Yessap was speaking again. 'Reckon that's Ed comin' now.' He began making a cigarette, face turned in an intent look down the trail.

A horseman suddenly appeared round the bend. Fanny stifled a gasp. Ed Manners, apparently keeping a rendezvous with the red-haired desperado. She could hardly believe her eyes. The newcomer's words dispelled any doubts.

'Hello, Red.' Manners extracted a cigar from vest pocket. 'What's the good word?' He chewed at the cigar, struck a match.

'Things is shapin' right smart,' Red Yessap answered. 'I've got a sure-fire play figgered out.'

Manners smiled, jerked a nod at the black-bearded man slouching in his saddle. 'You sure scared the life out of old Hendricks. Softened him up good, Vordal.'

'Far as I can see the thing went haywire,' grumbled Vordal. 'Softened Hendricks all right, but he went and sold the place to MacKenzie.'

'I'll take care of MacKenzie,' Manners said curtly. He climbed from his horse and with a beckoning nod to Yessap walked over to a flat boulder that lay at the foot of the opposite slope.

The two men sat there for some ten minutes in low-voiced conversation. Fanny caught snatches. *War Dance, Red Stone Corral.* An occasional laugh came from Manners. His voice, carried on the wind, came suddenly clear. 'Five thousand for MacKenzie and a fifty-fifty cut in the herd.'

Fanny was desperately frightened. Her first impulse had been to show herself to Manners. She was thankful for resisting the impulse. His friendliness with the man who had tried to kill Storm MacKenzie shocked her. Something was very wrong with Ed Manners.

The two men returned to their horses. Manners swung up to his saddle and looked at Vordal. 'You'll stick with Yessap until the thing's done.'

'Sure.' Vordal nodded. 'I'll git word to the other fellers. They'll want an even cut, though.'

'They'll get it,' Manners told him curtly.

'I'm gettin' a bonus for the job,' Red Yessap said. 'It was me thought out this play.'

'Sure,' agreed Manners. 'You're runnin' the show, Red. We've already talked the thing over and you've got my word for the bonus.'

'Word or no word, I'll be collectin' anythin' that's due me.' There was a threat in the outlaw's voice.

'Well, fellers—let's ride.' Yessap was suddenly in his saddle. There was something catlike about the little man. He sat there on his horse, making a cigarette and staring at Manners. 'Could have sworn you was waitin' here when we rode in from the gully. Sounded like a horse comin' down trail. Reckon it was only a rock-slide, like Vordal figgered.'

Throwing Manners a careless parting nod, the outlaw started his horse away. Vordal and Tonto trailed after him and in a few moments the trio vanished into the gully.

Fanny held her breath. It was plain that Yessap's words had disturbed Manners. He sat there on his horse, apprehensiveness visible in his roving gaze. Once his look fixed directly on her hiding place. The girl's heart skipped a beat.

Suddenly a clatter of falling stone broke the stillness. A small rock-slide from the opposite cliff. Fanny heard an abrupt exclamation from the man on the horse. In another moment he was riding away, down the canyon trail.

The girl let out a sigh of relief. She sat back on her heels. Her nerves had been strung taut and now that it was all over she felt undone—incapable of movement. For one terrifying moment she had been sure Manners was about to investigate the giant boulders that hid her. The slide of rocks down the cliff had saved her. It was like a miracle. A few falling stones had rescued her from an ugly dilemma. It *was* a miracle. Fanny knew she was always going to believe in miracles.

She got to her feet. Her knees felt stiff and sore. She stood there, rubbing out the aches and mustering courage to get back into the saddle and continue on her way to Mesalta. She dreaded an encounter with Ed Manners. He was riding toward town, too. She must be well out of the canyon in case they ran into each other. His suspicions would be aroused if he knew she had been up in the South Fork.

The gray horse cocked reproachful ears at her. Fanny gave him a grateful pat. She had been fearful that Baldy would do something to attract the attention of those men.

She climbed into the saddle and pushed on down the trail.

Manners must have ridden fast. Fanny saw no sign of him. At last she was out of the canyon and cutting across the piñon-covered mesa. The girl put the horse to a fast gallop, anxious to be home before the darkness set in.

Dave Stagg was lighting the big kerosene lamp that swung over the barn door when she turned in from the street. The old liveryman gave her a sharp look.

'You look some wore out,' he said.

'It's been a hard ride.' Fanny tried to speak lightly. She was longing to tell him about her strange encounter. There was something staunch about Dave Stagg, a kindly understanding. She ventured a question timidly.

76

'Has—has anything been heard of that man, Red Yessap?'

Dave shook his head. 'Hidin' out in some hole, like the wolf he is, I reckon.'

'He—he's really a bad man?'

'Don't come worse,' Dave said. 'Storm MacKenzie had him sent to jail for stealin' cows, but Red broke loose couple o' months back.'

'I should think they'd arrest him, send him back to prison.' Fanny gave the liveryman a troubled look. 'Why don't they arrest him?'

'Cain't catch him,' Dave told her laconically.

'I—I suppose Mr. MacKenzie was—was trying to catch him the other day when he killed the wrong man.'

'Reckon that's what started Red Yessap shootin',' admitted Dave dryly.

'I think it was terrible—Mr. MacKenzie killing the other man.' There was rising indignation in Fanny's voice. 'He seemed so—so callous about it.'

Dave looked at her curiously. 'I don't know just what that there word "callous" means, but if you're tryin' to make out that Stormy is kind o' *careless* with his shootin' irons you're sure barkin' up the wrong tree.'

'He didn't *seem* to care.' The girl's color mounted. She felt the liveryman was reproving her.

Dave shook his head soberly. 'Supposin' you was out alone some place, like you was this afternoon up in the South Fork, an' you'd a gun in your hand an' a wolf come rushin' you to git his fangs into your throat, wouldn't you use that gun on him doggone quick?'

'I—I suppose I would,' admitted Fanny. Her face paled. Yes, she would have used a gun on those men if she had fallen into their hands. Only she would have had no gun to use. Fanny made up her mind then and there to have a gun with her—next time.

'That's all Stormy done,' Dave Stagg went on. 'A pack o' wolves was rushin' him. Cain't blame him none for shootin' to kill. It come on him awful sudden. He done the best he could. Ain't his fault his bullet missed the king wolf.'

'It was terrible.' Fanny repressed a shiver.

'Sure was one close call for Stormy.' Dave's tone was solemn. 'There was two bullet holes in his Stetson, an' another one took a piece of skin off of his shoulder.'

She gave him an aghast look. 'He—he was wounded?'

'A scratch . . . nothin' worse'n a feller gits most any time he handles bob wire.'

'I'm afraid I'm a dreadful little tenderfoot.' Fanny's faint smile was apologetic. 'I've a lot to learn.'

The old ex-freighter nodded approvingly. 'When a feller admits he don't know much, he's the feller that can learn fast.'

'I can learn a lot from you,' Fanny said soberly. 'I've learned a lot already.'

'Come 'round any time you like,' cordially invited Dave. 'When you git 'round to it you'd learn lots from Sarah. She's got awful good sense, Sarah has.'

'You mean Mrs. Stagg?' Fanny smiled. 'I've noticed her on your hotel porch. She looks nice.'

'Sarah's got her good p'ints.' Dave chuckled. 'I tell her I wouldn't trade her off for the best team o' mules out of Missouri.'

'She ought to scalp you,' laughed the girl. She turned away reluctantly, still struggling with the urge to confide her disturbing experience. He was a wise old man, could advise her. A loud jangling of bells settled the matter.

'Sarah's callin' me to come an' git it or she'll throw supper away,' Dave said. 'When she bangs them old mule bells that's my special call.' His one eye gleamed reminiscently. 'Carried them bells on my lead team years back, when I was freightin' over the Santa Fe Trail.'

'I must hear more about those old days.' Fanny smiled.

'Can tell you some ha'r-raisin' tales,' chuckled Mr. Stagg. His face sobered, was suddenly grave as his look followed the girl's trim figure crossing the street. 'Got somethin' on her mind that worries her a lot,' he muttered.

In her room, Fanny made an attempt to think the matter out coolly. She sat on the bed, stared with unseeing eyes at the riding boot in her hand. Her mother tapped on the door.

'I'll be waiting down in the lobby, dear. Please hurry into your clothes. I'm starving—and Fanny, I've asked Mr. Manners to join us at our table.'

'I can't *bear* it!' Fanny's nerves were raw.

'What did you say, dear?'

'Nothing. Just thinking aloud.' Fanny spoke crossly. 'Don't wait dinner for me, Mother. I'm not sure I'll be down. I'm awfully tired from the ride.'

'Lester will be so disappointed,' remonstrated Mrs. Winston. She poked her head through the door. 'Why, child, you look so solemn, sitting there with one boot in your hand.'

'I told you I'm *tired.*' Fanny's tone was impatient. 'Please don't bother about me.'

'Where did you go?' persisted Mrs. Winston. 'Lester will want to know. He was saying he wished he could give you more of his time, but he is so dreadfully busy with the new sawmill.'

'Oh, up one of the canyons, some place they call the South Fork—' Fanny broke off, suddenly aghast at her carelessness. Ed Manners was having dinner with her mother and Lester. He would learn she had been in the South Fork. She was horrified, unpleasantly aware of a cold prickle of fear.

Mrs. Winston stared at her curiously. 'What's the matter, child? Such a queer look in your eyes.'

'Nothing's the matter with me, Mother, only I won't be down for dinner, if you don't mind.'

80

Mrs. Winston withdrew. She would explain to Lester and Mr. Manners, she promised. They would be so sorry.

Fanny glared at the closing door, tugged viciously at the remaining boot. She was furious with herself for her stupidly thoughtless answer. She could have cried. The fat was in the fire and no mistake. Ed Manners would prick up his ears when her prattling mother told them about the ride up the South Fork.

Her mind in a turmoil, Fanny slowly changed into a brown tweed suit. She really ought to tell somebody about Red Yessap. The man was wanted by the police, and yet, with her own eyes she had seen Ed Manners with him and apparently on friendly terms. She had heard enough to know that something was in the wind. Something to do with Storm MacKenzie.

The distracted girl suddenly found her thoughts on Lester Warde. After all, he was the man she should turn to. She was going to marry Lester. It was the natural thing to do, tell him the whole story of the mysterious meeting between Ed Manners and the notorious Red Yessap.

For some reason, Fanny recoiled from this solution. Lester Warde was apparently quite close to Ed Manners in a business way. He would pooh-pooh the whole thing. Also she shrewdly guessed that Lester had no liking for Storm MacKenzie. From several remarks she had overheard him make to Ed Manners, the girl gathered that Lester actually feared Storm MacKenzie as a threat to his lumber interests. Lester was not likely to care what happened to the young Diamond M man. There was something ruthless about Lester Warde. Fanny instinctively knew he was not the sort of man to be easily thwarted in his ambitions.

She went to the open window and looked down into the street. Two cowboys rode past with a musical jingle of spurs. She heard a voice hail them from the sidewalk.

'Hi, there, Jericho! How's things at the ol' Diamond M?'

'Fine as silk, Yuma. Be seein' you over at the Palace soon as we've et supper at Ma Stagg's.'

'Better come holdin' aces, feller. I'm feelin' some lucky tonight.'

The pair of Diamond M riders drifted on up the street toward the livery barn, flinging good-natured jibes over their shoulders at the unseen friend on the sidewalk.

Fanny's look went thoughtfully to the twin kerosene lamps winking from the porch of the Stagg House. The glimmer of an idea was taking shape in her mind. For some reason she was drawing comfort from the presence in town of those two happy-go-lucky Diamond M cowboys who were planning to eat their supper at Ma Stagg's. She felt a longing to talk to them. They were Storm MacKenzie's men and perhaps they would help her. She wanted desperately to see Storm MacKenzie.

Fanny reached for her hat, a small white Stetson, and made her way cautiously down the stairs. Nobody was in the lobby, save an elderly red-nosed man behind the desk. She hurried through, in another moment was crossing the street toward the Stagg House.

8
A Visit to the Palace Bar

THE two men halted their horses on the summit. Below them the lights of the town lay like a cluster of jewels on the dark blanket of the night.

Storm MacKenzie looked at his companion, slumped despondently in his saddle. 'Steep climb, Ben,' he said. 'Worth it when you're in a hurry. Saves five miles, this shortcut over the ridge.'

'The old mare ain't so good no more,' Hendricks complained. 'Ain't got the wind she used to have.'

'You should turn her out to pasture,' advised the younger man. 'She's carried you a lot of years.'

No response came from Hendricks and for a few moments there was a silence, touched only by the labored breathings of the winded mare.

Storm gloomily watched the winking lights. He intensely disliked the mission Ben Hendricks had prevailed upon him to undertake. He wished Ben had taken his tale of woe to some other person and not come out to the ranch bothering him with his troubles.

Hendricks broke the silence. 'Guess the mare's got her wind back, Stormy.'

The trail looped down in a series of steep pitches that brought sour comments from Ben. His bones had warped out of shape for sitting a saddle the way a man should, he told the younger rider.

'I'll be stove up for a week,' grumbled the old man. 'Wish I'd never sold Ponderosa. Was a fool to let them doggone Red Torchers scare me into sellin'.'

'You can go back there and live rent free, Ben.'

'If it wasn't for Louella I'd take you up on that deal.' Hendricks's tone was regretful. 'Guess I've lived with them yellow pines so long I ain't just feelin' to home no place else.'

'I've got to put a man up there to keep his eyes on things,' Storm told him. 'I'd pay you cowhand wages, Ben.'

'Guess it's goin' to be up to you, Stormy.'

'Louella, you mean,' Storm retorted.

'Wa'al, it's up to you to handle Louella . . . git the fool notions out of her head an' her off to some school in Phoenix.'

'Don't count on me,' grumbled the younger man. He gave his companion a sidewise look, was touched by the woebegone face. 'I'll do my best, Ben.'

'I know you will, Stormy. You're Jim MacKenzie's

son, an' Jim was never one to let a feller down. You're the spittin' image of him, Stormy.'

They off-saddled in front of the Palace Bar. Hendricks hesitated as Storm turned toward the swing doors. 'Guess I won't be goin' in with you, Stormy.'

'It's your business, and you're going in.' The young rancher's tone was firm.

Hendricks saw that protest was useless. 'Guess I can stand a shot o' whiskey at that,' he compromised. 'Mebbe take some o' the creaks out of my j'ints.' He followed his tall companion into the long barroom.

Storm led the way to a corner table where the lights were less glaring and crooked a beckoning finger at one of the barmen. The man picked up a bottle and glasses and brought them to the table.

'Ain't seen you for a coon's age, Mr. MacKenzie. Sure glad to see you.' The barman fondled the points of his enormous handlebar mustache, grinned hospitably. 'You've sure come to the right place for a good time. Got a little queen here that has the fellers standin' on their heads.'

Storm recognized him as a former chuck-wagon cook for the Diamond M outfit. 'Hello, Johnnycake. How come you've quit bossing a chuck-wagon for this business?'

Johnnycake waved a hamlike hand. 'Got too heavy for ridin' round in a doggone chuck-wagon.'

His grin widened. 'There's more money tendin' bar, speakin' the truth like a honest man.'

'You used to wear your mustache like a real cowman,' Storm bantered.

'A droopin' mustache don't look good on a bartender,' explained Johnnycake. 'What'll you have for a chaser, gents?' His tone was suddenly professional.

'Count me out,' smiled Storm. 'Ben, here, is the likker-hound tonight.'

'You never was one to care for likker,' chuckled Johnnycake.

'I take my poison straight,' Ben Hendricks said. 'Don't seem good sense to pay money for whiskey an' then pour water into it. You can git plenty water for nothin'.'

'Them is sound sentiments,' agreed Johnnycake with an approving smile. He turned away. Storm's voice halted him.

'Ask that girl to come over here, Johnnycake. The one with the yellow hair and green spangled dress.'

The fat barman's eyes bulged. 'You can sure pick 'em,' he admired. 'She's the new little queen I was tellin' you about.'

'I want to talk to her,' Storm said.

Ben Hendricks, hand clasped over the neck of the bottle, was staring angrily across at the dance floor. He suddenly banged the bottle loudly on the table. 'I've a mind to lay her acrost my knees an' spank her good.' His furious look went to the astonished barman. 'You tell her to come on the run, by cracky. Tell her it's her grandpa says so.' Hendricks tilted the bottle with a shaky hand, filled the glass, and tossed the contents down his throat. 'The hussy,' he fumed, 'wearin' that sinful dress, showin' her legs an' bosom, an' her face all painted like a doggone whore.'

The bartender was talking to Louella, thumb bent over shoulder in the direction of the corner table. Storm met her startled look. The girl was plainly disconcerted, and then she was suddenly pushing her way through the throng, chin defiantly up. A hulking lumberjack turned from the bar, glass in hand. He said something as she passed, reached out a paw to her smooth bare shoulder. Louella's hand swept up in a stinging slap that wiped the leer from his face. The man loosed an enraged oath, started after her.

Louella's grandfather, about to pour a second drink, popped up from his chair like a jack-in-the-box, hand clasped around the neck of the whiskey bottle. His arm swept out and the bottle hurtled through the air. It was a good throw, old Ben made. The bottle caught the lumberjack squarely on the forehead. He staggered, collided with a chair, and toppled to the floor.

Infuriated shouts followed the momentary hush. Several of the stricken man's companions surged toward the corner. Three cowboys came to their feet with a crash of overturned card table. Storm, already on his feet and reaching for his gun, recognized Jericho and Sooner. Their companion was a Lazy K man known as Yuma. The three were suddenly a compact wall in front of the charging lumberjacks. Guns bristled in their hands. The clattering booted feet halted abruptly.

The brief silence was broken by Sooner Bass. 'I'd sooner cut down a mangy woodchopper than eat.' All the bitterness felt by the cowman for the lumberjack was in his voice.

'Me, too, Sooner.' Jericho's eyes were pin-points of cold steel. 'Makes my trigger-finger ache any time I meet up with one of the coyotes.'

'Never could stand the sight of the axe-slingin' buzzards,' put in the Lazy K man. 'They got no bus'ness in this cow country.'

Johnnycake's belligerent voice interrupted further revilings. 'Now, gents . . . no brawlin'. Won't stand for this place gittin' messed up with dead folks. If you boys is cravin' to fight you can git out an' do your fightin' in the street.' Johnnycake was behind the bar, menacing shotgun in his hands.

Muttering threats, the lumberjacks helped their fallen comrade to his feet and guided his unsteady steps back to the bar.

Jericho's look went to the cards scattered under the upset table. Gloom spread like a dark cloud over his face. 'First royal flush I ever held,' he said

mournfully, 'an' there she lays on the floor. . . .
Come on, fellers. Let's git out of this joint. I ain't
got no more heart for poker tonight. I'm all broke
up, losin' my royal flush thataways.'

The trio started toward the door. Sooner halted.
'There's the boss.' Surprise was in his voice.
'Reckon we should tell him about that girl that was
talkin' to us over at Ma Stagg's.'

Jericho gripped his arm. 'Don't seem like a good
time, Sooner. He's got a girl with him . . . won't like
us bustin' in—' The cowboy broke off, stared with
bulging eyes. 'Doggone if she ain't Louella. . . .
Wasn't knowin' her a-tall in that fancy rig she's
wearin'.'

'Looks like she's havin' a row with her grandpa,'
muttered Sooner Bass.

' 'Twas her grandpappy threw the bottle,' the
Lazy K man told them. 'I seen the play. Frisky-
lookin' heifer,' he added appraisingly. 'Kind of
takes my fancy.'

Sooner Bass scowled. 'Don't git notions, Yuma.'

'What notions?' The Lazy K man pretended
indignation.

'Come on, fellers.' Jericho pushed out through
the swing doors.

Storm looked over in time to catch a covert
signal from Sooner. He guessed the cowboy had
something to tell him. The latter correctly inter-
preted his answering gesture. Sooner nodded,
pushed out to the street.

'The boss says for us to wait for him over at the Stagg House,' he informed Jericho.

Storm saw that Ben Hendricks was getting nowhere with his granddaughter. He said curtly: 'Let me do the talking, Ben. That's what I'm here for.'

Louella looked at him defiantly. 'I'm not carin' to listen, *Mister* Stormy MacKenzie.' She faltered, seemed suddenly abashed under his regard.

'I ain't standin' for it,' fumed Ben Hendricks. 'You come along with me an' wash that paint off of your face and git into some decent clothes.'

'I won't!' sulked the girl.

'Lettin' men put their hands on you,' grumbled the old man.

'I can take care of myself,' flared Louella. 'You saw what I did to that big fool when he tried to grab me.'

Storm spoke again. 'This is no place for you, Louella. I thought you planned to go to school.'

'I was over to Phoenix, lookin' round at schools. Kind of made me sick when I found out I'd have to sit with a lot of kids half my age.'

'You can use some of that money for a private teacher,' suggested Storm.

Louella set her mouth stubbornly. 'It's no use talkin',' she declared. 'I can make plenty money without learnin' things out of schoolbooks.'

'Ben was telling me.' Storm spoke grimly. 'Ed Manners is making a fool of you, Louella.'

'Ed's teachin' me the ropes. I'm goin' to run the games here for him. He says I'll be worth a hundred thousand inside of five years.'

'In the meantime you're to let him have the money I gave your grandfather for Ponderosa.' Storm's face darkened with anger.

'Fifteen thousand of it.' Louella's chin went up defiantly. 'It's my money. Grandpa gave it to me.'

'I said as how you could have it,' reluctantly admitted Ben, in response to Storm's inquiring look. 'You ain't got hold of it yet, though,' he added with a scowl. 'I give it to A. Solem to keep in his big safe until I said for him to turn it over to you.'

'I'm goin' to get it from him tomorrow,' declared the girl. 'I want Ed Manners to keep my money for me in his bank.'

Storm saw that it was hopeless. He looked at Ben, shook his head. 'Might as well be on my way. I can't stop her from playing the fool.'

Louella smiled disdainfully, stared at him under lowered lashes. Her hardness revolted Storm. He stood up.

'Let's get out of here, Ben—' He broke off, looked at the two men pushing in through the swing doors. The sight of them seemed to frighten Ben Hendricks. His long, gaunt frame rose with a startled movement that sent his chair over with a clatter.

'Ain't wantin' no ruckus with Ed,' he muttered.

Louella laughed triumphantly. 'Ed,' she called, 'come on over. You'll be sore as a boil when you hear what this nosey MacKenzie feller's been sayin' about you.' She slanted a vindictive glance at the Diamond M man, hands on slim hips, silver-slippered foot tapping the floor angrily.

'Now, Louella,' remonstrated Ben, 'you shouldn't go startin' a ruckus.'

There was a wary look in the saloon man's unsmiling eyes as he approached the corner table. Lester Warde trailed him. The lumberman gave Storm a chill nod.

'Reckon you can say it to my face, MacKenzie,' Ed began.

Ben Hendricks interrupted him. 'Now, Ed, don't you go listenin' to Louella's crazy talk.'

'I don't mind telling you, Manners.' Storm spoke quietly. 'Ben doesn't like Louella working in this dance hall of yours.'

'If you're smart, you'll mind your own business,' Manners said angrily.

'He says you're all set to steal my money,' broke in the girl.

The saloon man's face darkened. 'You're spreadin' yourself a lot, comin' to my place with your loose talk, MacKenzie.'

Storm's face was a mask. 'Not loose talk, Manners.'

Ed Manners looked at his companion, seemed to find something reassuring in the big man's unfriendly regard of Storm. 'You're a liar if you say I figger to steal Louella's money.'

'Why don't you throw the cow-walloper out on his neck?' Lester Warde laughed, looked at the girl for approval.

'You and who else?' queried Storm softly.

Warde's lip lifted in a grimace that showed broad white teeth. 'Nobody else needed, MacKenzie.' His tone was contemptuous. 'You cowmen think you own the country.'

Storm was watching the two men warily. Warde wore no gun, but the suspicious bulge of the saloon man's coat spoke of a concealed weapon.

Warde spoke again. 'Well, you heard me. Why don't you start something, cowboy?' His balled-up fist lashed out.

The blow caught Storm on the side of the head, careened him against the table. The lumberman was after him like a charging bull. Storm regained his balance, landed a left to the chin that halted Warde in his tracks. Storm struck again with his right and the big man staggered sideways, collided with Ben's fallen chair and sprawled his length.

Shouts came from the crowded bar. A bottle hurtled through the air, shattered against the wall behind Storm. A girl screamed from somewhere back on the dance-floor and suddenly the lumberjacks were rushing to the aid of their fallen boss.

Out of the corner of his eye Storm saw Ed Manners reaching inside his coat for the hidden gun. He jerked his own gun from holster. The saloon man hastily dropped his hand.

The sight of the long-barreled Colt brought the lumberjacks to a standstill. Behind them lifted Johnnycake's annoyed voice. 'Now, boys, I done just told you I ain't standin' for brawlin' in this bar.' The fat bartender's sawed-off shotgun was in his hands again. Manners gave him a venomous look that Johnnycake chose to ignore. Storm was his old-time boss, and Johnnycake felt there were occasions when cowmen must stand together. It was in the cards Ed would fire him. Johnnycake was not caring. He was suddenly aware of an urge to be again bossing a chuck-wagon.

Storm's look went to Lester Warde. The jarring fall had knocked the breath from him, but he was not really hurt. Storm gave old Ben Hendricks a nod. 'Let's go,' he said briefly. He started toward the door.

Ben paused to send his granddaughter a reproachful look. 'I'm sure cravin' to lay you acrost my knees,' he told her bitterly. 'You got a doggone good spankin' comin' to you, Louella.'

Johnnycake, wary eyes on the glowering lumber-jacks, sidled down the bar, spoke softly to Storm. 'Looks like I'll be huntin' a job ridin' a chuck-wagon, Stormy.'

'You're hired,' Storm told him. 'Barbecue wants to quit . . . says he's too old.'

'I'll be out to the ranch come next sundown.' The bartender's face glowed. 'Boss, you sure got guts—like old Jim's son *would* have.' His gaze shifted to the scowling lumberjacks, threatened them with hard, hostile looks.

'Come on,' Storm said to Ben. They pushed out into the starlight.

9
The Cabin in the Clearing

THE kerosene lamps still flared radiance in front of A. Solem's General Merchandise Emporium. Ben said in his dreary voice, 'Looks like A. Solem is workin' late.'

Something in his companion's hard stare across the street made Storm look at him. 'I know what's in your mind, Ben.'

'Sure.' Hendricks nodded. 'I've got a notion to git that money away from Solem before Louella goes an' talks him into handin' it over to her.' The old man loosed a dry cackle. 'Guess it'll give you a grin, Stormy. That there Armenian gent is gone awful sweet on Louella. He won't say no to her if she makes eyes at him.'

'She mustn't get that money.' Storm was worried. 'It's up to you, Ben.'

'I guess I can make Solem turn it back to me,' Ben admitted. 'Trouble is, Stormy, I'm kind o' no good at fightin' Louella. I can git that fifteen thousand away from A. Solem, but Louella will sure talk it out of me.'

Storm glowered at him. 'What kind of man are you, Ben?'

Ben shook his head sadly. 'Louella's too much for me, Stormy. She can always git the best of me. I ain't got no chance when she gits to ridin' me.'

As if drawn by their mutual thoughts the two men were crossing the dusty street toward the beckoning kerosene lamps that brightly lighted the wide porch in front of A. Solem's General Merchandise Emporium.

Storm said again, thoughtfully, 'She mustn't get that money, Ben.'

'Louella'll git it away from me,' repeated the old man in a troubled voice. He laid a hand on Storm's arm as they mounted the steps. 'Only thing to do, Stormy, is for me to hand that money over to you for safe-keepin'.'

'Let's talk to A. Solem.' The cowman's tone was noncommittal.

The storekeeper came hurriedly from his cubbyhole office. He'd kept open later than usual, he explained.

'I want the money I give for you to keep in your safe,' Ben told the Armenian bluntly.

A. Solem looked at him dubiously. 'I don't know as I can do that without Miss Louella's say-so, Ben. It's her money, and I'd want her say-so.'

'Ain't hers yet, not till I hand it over to her

myself,' argued Ben. 'Guess the money's still mine, A. Solem, an' I'm wantin' it now an' immediate.'

A. Solem's look questioned Storm. The rancher nodded. 'Ben's in the right, Solem. He hasn't actually turned that fifteen thousand over to the girl.'

The storekeeper hesitated, went reluctantly toward his big safe. 'If that's the way you see it, Mr. MacKenzie. Can't say I like handing it over this way. Don't seem fair to Miss Louella. She'll bawl me out good.'

'It's a sight o' money,' Ben said when Solem finished counting out the notes.

'Miss Louella won't like it,' Solem worried.

'She was fixin' to hand it over to Ed Manners,' explained Ben. 'You wouldn't want for her to be stole blind by *him,* would you?'

The storekeeper was visibly startled. 'I—I wouldn't say Ed would cheat her,' he stammered. His voice hardened. 'Wouldn't put it past him.'

'That's what Ben thinks,' smiled Storm.

Hendricks stood staring at the big wad of bills clutched in his hand. 'No sense me keepin' this stuff,' he muttered. 'Louella'll git it away from me sure as Monday follows Sunday. I ain't got the wits to match her no more.' His look went to Storm. 'Guess it's up to you, Stormy. She won't be gittin' it away from you.'

'I'll take care of it for you, Ben,' agreed Storm. He pushed the wad of notes into a pocket. 'Well, *adios*, Solem.'

97

'You will stay the night in town?' queried the storekeeper. He was staring hard at Storm's hands.

The latter shook his head. 'Got to get back to the ranch. Awfully busy these days.'

'You've got blood on your hands!' A. Solem exclaimed. 'Your knuckles are bleeding, Mr. MacKenzie.'

Ben Hendricks winked knowingly at the curious-eyed owner of the Emporium. 'Guess that Warde feller can tell you about them knuckles if he's a mind to, Solem,' cackled the old man.

A. Solem's misgivings grew as he went about the business of closing up the store. He pulled the chains of the porch kerosene lamps and stood staring thoughtfully across at the brightly lighted front of the Palace Bar. Ben Hendricks's comment about Lester Warde was not hard to interpret. The answer to Storm MacKenzie's bruised knuckles was plain enough. Blows had passed between the cattleman and the lumberman.

The storekeeper liked Storm MacKenzie, but prudence forbade an alliance with the rancher against the powerful lumber interests. It was obvious he had made a grave mistake in letting Ben Hendricks turn all that money over to Storm MacKenzie. It seemed that Lester Warde was in some way involved with Ed Manners in this matter of Louella's money. Not only Manners would be down on him like a ton of bricks, but he would have incurred the more-to-be feared wrath of the powerful lumberman.

A. Solem came to a quick decision. He must make a clean breast of the affair to Manners and Warde. He could even intimate that Storm had threatened to use his gun, had actually forced him to hand over the money.

The storekeeper started across the street, conscious of a mounting indignation as he mentally rehearsed his story. No doubt but what Storm MacKenzie *would* have used his gun, forced him to open the safe. Solem's fairy tale took on the dark outlines of sinister reality as he pushed through the swing doors of the Palace Bar.

Storm found Sooner Bass and Jericho swapping yarns with Dave Stagg in the hotel lobby. The latter looked at him, a hopeful gleam in his one good eye. 'Hello, Stormy. You stayin' here tonight?'

Storm shook his head. 'Got to be on my way back to the ranch. Only stopped in to find out what Sooner has on his mind.' His eyes questioned the two cowboys.

'A girl come in while Jericho an' me was eatin' supper,' Sooner Bass told him. 'We wasn't knowin' her a-tall, but Ma Stagg says she wears the name o' Winston an' lives over at the Palace with her ma.'

Dave Stagg nodded confirmation. 'The Winston

girl,' he said. 'Ma was tellin' me she come in after I'd done et supper an' gone back to the barn. Right nice young female,' Dave added emphatically.

Storm's face gave no hint of the sudden stirring of his pulse. 'What about her, Sooner?'

Jericho stifled an amused laugh. 'Looks like she's swingin' a rope for you, boss.'

Sooner Bass gave him a hard look. 'Shut up, feller. Ain't you got sense in that sandy top of yours?'

Dave Stagg said soberly: 'From what the boys was tellin' Sarah an' me, the Winston girl is awful set on havin' a talk with you, Stormy. Somethin' on her mind that worries her plenty.'

Sooner Bass nodded. 'She's sure one worried girl, boss. Was askin' the best way to git word to you. We wasn't knowin' you'd be in town tonight. Wasn't knowin' you was here till we seen you over in the Palace Bar.'

'I can't wait over to see her,' Storm said. 'Wonder what's up?'

'She come in this evening from a ride up the South Fork,' Dave Stagg confided. 'Seemed awful nervous, was askin' questions about Red Yessap.'

Storm's eyes widened in a startled look at him.

'Somethin' happened up in the South Fork that sure scared her plenty,' Dave declared. 'Reckon you should stay over an' have a talk with her, Stormy. Way I figger the thing it concerns you.'

Storm shook his head. He couldn't possibly stay. He had to get back to the ranch. He was thinking of the thick roll of bills in his pocket. He wanted to be out of Mesalta before Louella heard the news from A. Solem.

'I'll be back in town in a day or two,' he compromised. 'You slip Miss Winston the word, Dave, if you get a chance.'

The liveryman agreed. 'She comes round to the barn most every day. Likes to go ridin'.'

Storm's troubled mind fastened on the problem of Red Yessap. 'What's Yuma doing here in town?' His look went to the two Diamond M men.

'Ain't knowin' for sure.' Jericho shook his head. 'We kind of got the notion Kendall sent him over on some sort of scout for Red Yessap.'

'Yuma's awful close-mouthed,' put in Sooner Bass. 'He don't talk free about Lazy K bus'ness, but somethin' he let slip give Jericho an' me the notion that he's huntin' sign for Yessap.'

' 'Twas Yuma give me the news about Red breakin' loose from jail,' reminded Dave. 'I was tellin' you the other day, you'll remember, Stormy.'

Storm nodded. Pete Kendall, the owner of the Lazy K, had been in town, too, he recalled.

Dave Stagg seemed to divine his thoughts. 'Pete Kendall's got a reward hung up for Red Yessap. Pete claims 'twas Yessap killed a Lazy K feller . . . sneaked up on him in camp an' shot him in the back. Looks like Red was wantin' this line rider's horse an' grub.'

Jericho and Sooner Bass made harsh noises in their

throats, exchanged grim looks. They were thinking of Wally Stevens, found shot in the tule swamp.

'I'd sure like to meet up with this Red Yessap,' growled Sooner Bass.

'Sure would,' rasped Jericho. 'No reward wanted, you can bet. All we want is just a chance to fix him the way he fixed Wally.'

'You two boys are heading back to camp tonight,' decided Storm. 'Things don't look good and I want you to stick close to Jim Race.'

They hid their disappointment with careless grins. 'Looks like you're the loser, Dave,' chuckled Jericho. 'Won't be needin' your beds tonight. All right, Sooner. Let's ramble over to the barn and git our prancin' steeds.'

Dave sent out a parting shot. 'Watch yourselves, young fellers. Them broncs of yours will likely make you play peekaboo with the stars, now they got a good feed in 'em.'

'Maybe we'll bring you a nice little shiny star to pin on your shirt,' retorted Jericho over his shoulder.

Dave chuckled. 'Always gets the last word, that kid.'

'Wouldn't be a bad idea at that,' said Storm.

'Meanin' what?' queried Dave Stagg.

'A star on your shirt, a sheriff's star.'

'I'm too old an' stove up,' protested Dave. 'Anyway, won't be another election for most a year.'

'Now's the time to make plans,' argued Storm. 'We don't want Vin Terrill for sheriff again, Dave.'

Dave looked down his bony nose. 'There's talk that Terrill's ranch is mortgaged awful heavy.'

'And Ed Manners holds the mortgage.' Storm got out of his chair. 'Well, *adios*—'

'You should let me fix you up with a fresh horse,' suggested the liveryman.

Storm agreed. He'd left his horse tied at the hitch-rail in front of the saloon, he told Dave.

'We'll go get him,' Dave said. 'Seen you when you rode in with Ben,' he added. 'Ben looked some worried.' The liveryman wagged his head. 'Reckon he's got cause, the way that Louella acts up. She's sure a wild one . . . all set to be a high-stepper.' Dave snorted. 'Claims the Stagg House ain't good enough for the likes of her. Got old Ben livin' over to the Palace Hotel. Ben's sure one poor bleatin' maverick these times.' Storm's grim silence discouraged the liveryman. He got out of his chair. 'Well, let's git your brown horse over to the barn, an' you hittin' the trail for the ranch.'

Three men watched them from the dark alley between the saloon and the Palace Hotel.

'It's the truth, Ed.' A. Solem spoke thickly. Whiskey always caught his tongue. 'It's the way I told you. What could I do, with his gun at my head?'

'Leave it to me, Solem. Smart of you to wise us up to this play MacKenzie put over on you.'

Lester Warde gingerly touched his sore chin. 'We've got to stop him, Ed.'

'Leave it to me,' repeated Manners.

Warde fingered his aching chin. 'I'm going over there to the barn and jump him myself.'

'You keep out of this deal,' counseled Manners. 'I've already got a plan figgered out. You take A. Solem back in the bar for a drink on the house.'

He waited until the others disappeared into the saloon, then went quickly along the alley and turned up the hill that overlooked the town. Several small dilapidated log cabins clung to the steep slope. Manners passed them, pushed deeper into the thick tangle of stunted junipers, and halted at the door of a cabin that stood alone in a clearing. There was a shed, and several horses in a pole corral.

Alert ears had already detected Manners's arrival. The door was suddenly jerked open, revealed Vordal against the glow of the lamp on a table. Manners stepped inside, nodded at the three men playing cards. They looked up inquiringly.

'Got a job for you,' Manners said. He lowered himself into a chair. The quick steep climb had taken his wind.

'A ridin' job?' queried Vordal.

'Quick as you can get started,' Manners told him. 'Won't need more 'n a couple of you.'

Vordal's look went to one of the card-players. 'You go throw on a couple of saddles.'

The man clattered out. 'All right, boss.' Vordal took the vacated chair. 'Let's hear what's on your mind.'

10
Wits Against Guns

THE big brown horse followed freely on his lead-rope. Storm had been reluctant to leave him back in Dave Stagg's barn. He had cared for Cacique himself from the horse's yearling days and gentled him to the saddle. Cacique had never felt another man on his back.

The horse supplied by Dave was a good enough animal, which was no surprise for Storm. Dave got most of his horses from the Diamond M. The ranch was famous for good saddle stock.

The late moon was well up by the time the fast-moving rangy bay made the steep climb to the summit of the first ridge and struck across the juniper-covered flats. A gray shape drifted across the trail, brought a snort from the bay horse. The coyote halted on a rocky hillock some twenty yards from the trail, took a brief backward look before slithering into the concealing darkness of the brush.

The sight of the little prowler dragged Storm from a momentary abstraction. No time to be mooning along when Red Yessap might be skulking behind some boulder. There could be no letdown of vigilance while the man continued to run loose.

Storm's perturbed thoughts went to the Winston

girl. If Dave Stagg's surmise was correct something had happened to frighten her. She had been riding up in the South Fork, according to Dave. It was possible she had stumbled on some clue to Yessap's hiding place. Miss Winston would have got a good look at the man that afternoon in Mesalta. She was not likely to forget him. Yessap and his companions had almost run the girl down as they tore past, their guns blazing at him.

The young cattleman's brows drew down in a perplexed frown. If the girl had accidentally run into Yessap it would be the natural thing for her to speak of it to Lester Warde. The man was her fiancé. And there was Ed Manners, in whose hotel she was a guest. Or she could have told Dave Stagg. Obviously she had preferred to make it a secret for some reason. The thing simmered down to only one answer. The girl was afraid to confide in Warde or Manners, and it was probable she was not sure how far she could go with Dave Stagg.

The trail reached out in a straight line across the juniper flats. The lifting moon touched the harsh branches with silvered tips of light. A big hoot owl rose from a scraggly dead stump, drifted into the night on soundless wings. Cacique pulled up alongside with his easy running walk that kept the bay moving at a jog trot. Suddenly the big brown gelding's head went up, ears twitching nervously back.

Storm gave him a sharp look, immediately pulled

off the trail and drew rein behind a thick clump of junipers.

Stillness settled. Storm sat there in his saddle, ears sharpened to catch the sound that had aroused Cacique. He had learned to have respect for the brown horse's signals.

Presently he picked up the sound, the unmistakable clink of shod hoofs against stone. The young cattleman's face hardened, and after a moment he swung from his saddle and gave Cacique an affectionate slap on the neck. Thanks to the alertness of the brown horse, the unknown riders following the trail would not catch him unawares.

Because of the steep approach at either end, the Juniper Flats trail was seldom used except as a shortcut by those having business at the Diamond M Ranch. It was a hard trail, but it saved a good five miles for a man who did not mind rough going and was in a hurry.

For very good reasons, Storm suspected the intentions of the approaching horsemen. He knew of no person who would be riding from Mesalta to the ranch at so late an hour. Jim Race and his Diamond M crew were working the cedar brakes, and Jericho and Sooner would not think of getting back to the outfit's camp on Cedar Creek by way of the juniper flats.

Storm was curious to learn the identity of the riders trailing him. He believed he could name one of them. Red Yessap, and Red Yessap meant a bullet in the back when a convenient lonely trail offered a safe ambush. It was not probable that the stalking killers would make an attempt until the trail left the wide stretch of Juniper Flats. They would wait until Storm was climbing the steep gorge of Los Gatos Canyon. They could make a quick detour by way of Two Indian Peaks and lie in wait for him as he rode into Dead Man's Pass.

A wary look back trail told him the horsemen were still beyond the bend, less than an eighth of a mile distant. The clink of shod hoofs on stones came to him plainly, warned him he must act swiftly.

In a moment he had the tie-rope slipped from Cacique's neck. The brown horse jumped forward with an indignant snort as he felt the sting of the rope across his sleek flanks. In another instant the animal was heading for the ranch on the dead run.

Storm knew the horse would not stop until he was back at the Diamond M corrals. It was the way of a horse to make a bee-line for the home ranch. The only home Cacique knew was the Diamond M.

Storm drew back into the covering brush. The sound of Cacique's galloping hoofs broke sharply through the night, and suddenly from the lower side of the flats rose the drumming hoofbeats of pursuing horses.

They came on swiftly, vague, fast-moving shapes in the pale light of the lopsided moon.

Storm froze back in the dark shadows of the junipers, closed a hand firmly over the bay's nose. There was a chance that excited by Cacique's abrupt leave-taking and the onrush of the strange horses, the bay might let out a nicker.

The two riders tore past, neck and neck. Storm, watching from the screening branches, was conscious of a sharp shock of surprise. He could see the men clearly. One of them was a stranger, a short, stocky man with a broad, brutish face, and a gun in his free hand. His companion was certainly not Red Yessap. He wore a heavy dark beard. Storm's eyes narrowed. He knew the bearded man, had seen him hanging around the Palace Bar.

The sound of the chase drew swiftly away across the flats. Storm had no fears for the brown horse. Cacique was fast, well able to keep beyond possible pistol shot. Also pursuit would frighten the horse to top speed.

There was a certain grim humor in the situation. Storm could have laughed if he had not been so angry. It would not be long before the would-be killers discovered they were chasing a riderless and saddleless horse. Their surprise would be complete. They would be a pair of very puzzled men.

Storm's face took on a grim look as he stood there. He was beginning to understand the attempt of these men to bushwhack him. The black-bearded man was Vordal, and according to Dave Stagg, was a member of the notorious Red Torch gang. Storm felt he had the answer. These men had been sent to destroy him because of his recent purchase of the Palos Verdes hills from old Ben Hendricks.

Whatever the answer, Storm was certain that his life was being sought. He got into his saddle, rode a short hundred yards to another thick tangle of junipers that grew close to the trail. He suspected the two men would soon be heading back for Mesalta. They would not continue a senseless chase of a stray horse. They would be riding back, puzzled over the disappearance of the man they had been trailing.

Storm looked thoughtfully at the gun in his hand. The advantage of surprise should be *his* this time. The pair would not suspect he would be waiting for them with gun ready. The chances were in his favor.

The thought of Ben's fifteen-thousand-dollar bankroll in his pocket disturbingly arose. It was all right to risk his own life in attempting to capture Vordal and his companion, but if things went wrong, Ben would lose his money.

The young rancher glowered through the scraggly junipers at the open stretch of trail beyond. He could not afford a possible blunder at this time, not with old Ben's money in his keeping. And then suddenly he saw the two men, coming back down the trail, winded horses moving at a slow, shuffling walk.

Storm slid from his saddle, again clamped a hand over the nose of the bay horse. He stood there, gun ready in his free hand. If the worst came, he would shoot—shoot to kill.

The riders drew up slowly. It was obvious their horses were played out—the hard climb up from the Mesalta side and the furious spurt after the fast-moving Cacique. It was plain, too, that the men were in a disgruntled mood. Their voices came distinctly.

'Looks like we sure got the wrong tip.' Storm recognized Vordal's growly voice. 'MacKenzie never come this way. What we figgered was his horse was nothin' but that stray bronc.' Vordal added a string of epithets so vilely descriptive of Cacique that Storm's trigger-finger tightened wrathfully.

'Sure lit out hell-bent-for-election when he heard us closin' up on him,' chortled Vordal's companion. 'Never see a bronc git up speed so quick like that stray did.'

'Must have been one of Dave Stagg's broncs,' was Vordal's canny guess. 'Dave gits most of his stock from the Diamond M, an' them Diamond M horses can run like blazes. This stray must have broke loose an' was headed back to the ranch.'

'Wonder where MacKenzie got to?' The stocky man's tone was querulous. 'The boss sure slipped up bad, tellin' us MacKenzie was takin' the shortcut across the flats.'

Storm strained his ears for Vordal's answer, impatient for some clue as to the identity of the 'boss.' The riders were drawing away and he only faintly caught the man's words, smothered by the shuffling hoofs of the horses, the jingle of spurs, and creak of saddle leather.

'. . . ain't one to git things mixed . . . looks like he done figgered wrong. . . . MacKenzie must have took the long road . . . I'm sure—' The words trailed away in a blast of profanity.

Storm waited until the unpleasant pair had passed from sight around the bend. Presently the muffled hoofbeats died away in the distance and silence again brooded over the flats.

Finally he swung back into his saddle and started the bay horse up the trail toward the winding ascent of Los Gatos Canyon. His thoughts were troubled as he rode, turned to wild speculations. *Was Red Yessap the mysterious boss?* Storm rejected this solution, finally gave up trying to answer the question. Of one thing only was he certain. Red Yessap was not alone in his feud with the owner of the Diamond M Ranch. There were other, equally sinister, men who sought his life.

He kept the bay horse pounding along, allowed his thoughts to stray to the Winston girl. There was something completely stirring in the knowledge that she was apparently concerned for his safety.

11
A Dangerous Secret

THE financial transactions of the Pioneer Bank were confined almost entirely to its owner's personal business. There were no checking accounts, and the few depositors merely held Ed Manners's receipt for money entrusted to his big safe. Ed was the institution's president, cashier, and teller. He kept hours to suit his own convenience. Most of his customers were lumberjacks who knew they could find him in the Palace Bar. More often than not this first port of call made it a sure thing for Ed. His would-be depositors' money eventually reached the bank's coffers by way of the bar and gaming tables. This method simplified the banking business for Ed.

The big profits from his saloon were making bigger profits from many varied and unscrupulous enterprises. There were ranch mortgages in his safe that would never be paid off. Ed was gradually accumulating a large acreage in the Little Mesalta country.

He sat at his desk, placed to give him a view of the street through the famous plate-glass window. A document was spread out in front of him. Ed carefully scrutinized the signature, picked up a magnifying glass and compared it letter for letter with the name scrawled on a sheet of paper he extracted from a drawer.

The result of the comparison seemed to satisfy him. He leaned back in his chair and lighted a cigar. The forgery was a masterpiece, the best he'd ever done, would even fool Storm MacKenzie.

The thought seemed to amuse Ed Manners. His lip lifted in a hard little smile. Storm MacKenzie would never have a chance to see the signature to the quitclaim deed that in due time was to give Ed undisputed possession of the Diamond M Ranch. Storm MacKenzie would be dead.

Ed carefully replaced the small sheet of paper in its envelope. It was Storm's written and signed agreement to give him a quitclaim deed to the Palos Verdes pines in the event of failure to pay the ninety-day note. The agreement really was the property of Lester Warde. The lumberman had put up the twenty thousand dollars Ed had loaned to young MacKenzie.

Manners's lip lifted in the same little hard smile. Warde had been after him for the agreement, but Ed had other ideas. No sense in letting Warde get his hands on that yellow pine. MacKenzie would be a dead man before the note fell due, and if the agreement should happen to be lost there was nothing to prevent Ed from possessing Ponderosa along with the Diamond M. Warde could whistle for his twenty thousand dollars, say good-bye for ever to his hopes of some day logging the Palos Verdes slopes. Not unless he cared to raise the ante. That yellow pine was worth all of a hundred thousand.

He put the agreement and the forged quitclaim deed away in his safe. Both were worthless unless his plans matured.

Manners chewed viciously on his cigar. MacKenzie was a wary customer. The affair of the previous night was proof that he carried his wits with him, was a fast worker. He'd made a fool of Vordal.

The saloon man scowled. He was far from satisfied with Vordal's tale. Ed was positive Storm had taken the Juniper Flats trail for the ranch. Vordal swore he hadn't, claimed he and Ducker had found themselves following a stray horse and that Storm must have taken the long road home. Storm had managed to pull a smart trick on Vordal. Ed was sure of it.

A reassuring thought comforted Manners. He had not yet played his ace card. Last night's affair was only an unexpected chance to make a quick end of MacKenzie. Nobody would have guessed the truth. Another killing in Dead Man's Pass. Well-known cattleman drygulched and robbed of a large sum of money entrusted to him by a friend. Leave it to old Ben Hendricks to spread the story.

Manners pursed his lips thoughtfully. Red Yessap would finish the job. No chance for a failure when a man hated Storm MacKenzie the way Red Yessap hated him.

The Winston girl was crossing the street. Manners watched her from his desk chair. She was a good-looker. He didn't like her, but was forced to admit she was worth a closer view than he could get through his plate-glass window; also he wanted to talk to the girl.

His face darkened. The Winston girl had been riding up in the South Fork, according to her mother's story. There was just a chance she might have seen him.

Manners was conscious of a disquieting prickle of fear. It was even possible the girl had seen more than was good for her to see. Perhaps she had seen him talking to Red Yessap.

He waited for a moment, long enough to let suddenly taut lines in his face relax. No sense in frightening the girl, allowing her to see his apprehensions. He forced a smile, looked approvingly at his reflection in the small mirror on the wall, reached for his wide-brimmed hat and sauntered into the street.

Fanny Winston showed no sign of her own apprehensiveness as she saw him approaching. She was on her way to the livery barn to get her horse, she told Manners.

'You should try Red Canyon,' he advised. 'Good trail up the South Fork, and you can get a view of the Painted Desert from the rimrock.' Manners smiled. 'Long way off, though, the Painted Desert. Couldn't get there in a day's ride.' He was watching her closely. 'Reckon I ain't needin' to tell you, now I come to think of it.' He chuckled. 'Your mother was tellin' Les Warde an' me you was up in the South Fork in the afternoon. Clean forgot she was tellin' us you was up there.'

The girl's eyes widened. 'Mother told you *that?*' Fanny laughed. 'I'm afraid Mother got things mixed up.' She wondered if the man detected the slight tremor in her voice. He was staring at her so intently.

Manners nodded. 'Sure she told us, said you'd been up in the South Fork an' was too tired to come down to supper.'

Fanny shook her head. 'I suppose she heard me talking about trying the South Fork some day, but it's not very important, Mr. Manners.' She smiled. 'Thank you, though, for telling me about the Painted Desert view. I really must ride up there very soon.'

'Well worth the trip,' declared Mr. Manners in a too hearty voice, and politely tipping his hat he turned into the barber shop.

Fanny continued on her way to the livery barn. She was aware of an odd fear constricting her heart.

Dave Stagg gave her a shrewd look as she came up to where he stood in front of the wide doors of the livery barn. Fanny smiled, peered into the shadowy depths, down the long line of stalls. She delighted in the homey sound of the horses crunching their hay and oats.

'It always seems so peaceful here,' she said to

Dave. Her look went to a big freighting outfit in one of the corrals. 'Those huge wagons thrill me. I often wonder where they come from and where they are going.'

'That's Baldy Simpson's outfit,' Dave told her. 'Baldy makes the haul from Prescott to Albuquerque.'

Fanny watched the tall, lanky teamster at work with his long hitch of mules. He went about hooking them into line with an unhurried efficiency that fascinated her. She could hear his quietly admonishing voice. 'Hi, Maud, mind that chain, you lop-eared she-devil. You, Fanny, git over thar, doggone you.' The steady stream of soft-spoken words sounded like an oft-repeated monologue.

The girl gave Dave an amused look. 'The idea! Calling one of his mules by *my* name.'

Dave chuckled. 'Never did saw a mule hitch that hadn't a Maud an' a Fanny. Them names kind of fit a span o' mules natural-like.'

'They mind him well,' said Fanny. 'They seem to understand what he says.'

'Mules is next thing to human,' Dave commented dryly. He was watching her sharply. The girl's apparent interest in the freighter and his mules was not fooling him. She was pale and her eyes showed signs of sleepless hours. 'Storm MacKenzie was in last night.' His tone was purposely casual.

'You mean he—he went away again?' Fanny's face clouded. 'I was dreadfully wanting to see him.'

'Jericho an' Sooner Bass was tellin' him about you,' Dave said.

'They gave him my message?'

Dave nodded. 'Storm couldn't wait over to see you. He's awful rushed at the ranch.' He gave her a troubled look. 'Jericho was sayin' you're all scared 'bout somethin'.'

'I am,' confided the girl.

He continued to probe her cautiously. 'Somethin' that you maybe run into up in the South Fork?'

Fanny hesitated. She was wondering how far she could trust the old liveryman. 'You've been here a long time, Mr. Stagg. You know everybody, don't you?'

'Been here a spell o' years,' admitted Dave. 'Reckon I'm 'quainted with most all the folks within a hundred miles an' more.'

'You know Mr. Manners? I mean all about him?'

'Ed Manners is 'bout as mean as they make 'em.' Dave's drawling voice took on a harder note. 'Ed ain't been in Mesalta so long—maybe three years. He's a pizen rattlesnake, for all his smooth talk.' The liveryman shook his head. 'I'd sooner trust a rattlesnake.'

'Oh.' Fanny's face took on an added paleness. 'I don't like him, either, Mr. Stagg.'

119

'Seen you talkin' to him in front of the barber shop as you come along.' Dave's tone was mildly questioning.

'Mr. Stagg'—Fanny's voice was panicky—'don't tell him I was up in the South Fork yesterday afternoon.'

'I don't tell Ed Manners nothin' when he comes askin' questions,' Dave said dryly. He chewed reflectively on his tobacco cud. 'You mean Ed craves to know where you went ridin' yesterday?'

'He—he seems a bit curious,' answered the girl in a low voice.

Dave looked at her steadily, and there was a kindly gleam in his one eye. 'I ain't one to ask questions myself,' he said simply.

'I—I'm dreadfully worried.' Fanny spoke unhappily. 'I really must see Mr. MacKenzie.'

'Some talk that you're goin' to marry the Warde feller,' drawled Dave. 'You could go tell him what's on your mind.'

The color mounted in her smooth cheeks. 'I've thought of it,' she admitted. 'I—I really don't know, Mr. Stagg. You see, Lester is a friend—I mean a business friend—of Mr. Manners.' Fanny shook her head. 'I'm not sure I'd be doing right—if I told Lester.'

'If it's anythin' to do with Storm MacKenzie you could tell me.' Dave spoke bluntly. 'Stormy's my friend. I knowed his dad afore the boy was born. Stormy's four-square—a man to ride the river with. Don't nobody come better than Stormy MacKenzie.'

'That's high praise,' Fanny said, coloring again for some reason.

Dave noticed the wave of color, gave her a quick, shrewd look. 'I ain't praisin' him.' He spoke soberly. 'I'm givin' you the truth. Stormy's friends'd go to hell for him.'

The girl scarcely heard. She was recalling again her first glimpse of Storm MacKenzie as she peeped through the rain curtains of the rocking stage. The impact of his look, the quiet efficiency of him, the easy grace of tall, strong body. Odd, how that moment remained so vividly alive with her.

She was suddenly conscious of hot cheeks, of Dave Stagg's quizzical regard. 'I'm glad you say things like that about him.' She gave the liveryman a shy smile. 'It makes me feel all the more'— Fanny floundered, colored again—'I mean I feel he should know about what I saw up in the South Fork yesterday afternoon.'

'I figgered you'd run into somethin' up there.' Dave nodded. 'You was awful upset when you come back to the barn.'

Fanny was silent, her face pale again, warm brown eyes dark with indecision.

'Maybe I can help you,' Dave encouraged gently. 'Stormy's my friend. Nothin' I wouldn't do for Stormy.'

Fanny took the plunge. 'I saw that man—Red Yessap. The man who tried to kill Mr. MacKenzie, here in the street.'

Dave stared at her. It was obvious he was startled by the disclosure. His grizzled brows drew down in a worried frown. 'Don't blame you for bein' scared. Red's a pizen-mean customer.'

'He didn't see me,' Fanny reassured him. 'I hid behind two big boulders where I could watch, really a butte that had split in two, making a crevice that gave me a safe peephole. Two other men rode in with Yessap from a small gully.' She gave Dave Stagg a picture of the scene, beginning with the warning from the gray horse.

Dave listened, refraining from comment until the girl finished describing those first moments of alarm.

'You wouldn't be knowin' the other fellers,' he finally observed.

'One of them had a black beard,' Fanny told him.

'Huh! Shouldn't be s'prised if he was a feller by the name of Vordal. He wears a black beard, an' a heart that's blacker.' Dave's tone was grim.

'I think the other man was with Yessap when they tried to shoot Mr. MacKenzie here in the street.' Fanny repressed a shiver. 'Those faces seem stamped in my mind.'

Dave nodded, waited for her to continue. He sensed there was more to come.

'A fourth man rode up from the lower canyon,'

the girl went on. 'I was terribly shocked, Mr. Stagg.'

'Maybe I can guess who this feller was.' Dave's tone was grave. 'If the feller wearin' the black beard was Vordal, this other feller'd likely be Ed Manners. This Vordal feller is a sort of jackal to Manners.'

'You're clever to guess.' Fanny smiled faintly. 'Yes, this last man was Mr. Manners.'

'Sure looks bad,' muttered the old liveryman. 'Ed's reckoned to be a honest citizen in this town. Honest folks don't hold secret pow-wows with renegades like Red Yessap.' Dave snorted. 'Don't s'prise me none, him consortin' with rustlers an' such. Always did figger he was no good.'

'It's all very strange and frightening,' Fanny said. 'This man Yessap is a fugitive from prison, and Mr. Manners was as friendly as could be with him.' Her pallor returned. 'You can't blame me for being afraid of him when he tried to pump me about the South Fork.' Her tone was rueful. 'I told Mother about the ride and I'm afraid she mentioned it to Mr. Manners.'

Dave was frankly troubled. 'Too bad she told him. Ed'll likely think you seen him talkin' with Yessap.'

'He's up to something bad.' Fanny related the snatches of conversation.

'The War Dance, huh?' Dave's eyes narrowed thoughtfully. 'Old Apache trail, the War Dance.

Some folks still call that stone corral War Dance. The Injuns used to make big medicine there when they was goin' on the warpath.' He shook his head. 'Looks bad, this talk you heard. The Diamond M use that place for workin' cattle, call it Red Canyon Corral.'

'I'm sure there's some plot against Mr. MacKenzie,' worried the girl.

'You could have told me yesterday,' Dave said a bit gruffly.

She flushed. 'I—I wasn't quite sure—about you.'

'Reckon you're sure now.' His smile forgave her.

'Yes,' Fanny said simply. 'I'm sure—very sure—now.'

Dave returned to Ed Manners. 'What did you tell him when he asked if you'd been ridin' up the South Fork yesterday?'

'I'm afraid I fibbed.'

'Should-a sworn up an' down you wasn't near the place,' grumbled the liveryman. 'Got a notion Ed wasn't swallerin' your fib a-tall.'

'He *did* give me a queer look,' admitted the girl. She was suddenly panicky. 'Oh, Mr. Stagg! Supposing he learns that I saw him with Red Yessap? I was really frightened, the way he looked at me.'

'It's bad business,' muttered Dave Stagg. His expression was grim. 'Ed Manners won't like you knowin' his secret. No tellin' what he'll do.'

'There's the sheriff,' began the girl nervously.

124

Dave snorted. 'Ed owns the sheriff down to the last acre of his ranch. The sheriff won't take your word 'gainst Ed's. No use goin' to the sheriff. He won't do nothin', save give you the laugh.'

The ponderous freight wagons were pulling away from the corrals, Baldy Simpson in the saddle on one of the powerful wheel horses. His quiet voice came to them, curt, exhorting words to the long mule-hitch hooked in front of the wheelers. Bells jangled musically on the lead team as the outfit rumbled up the street.

Dave Stagg lifted a hand in a parting salute. 'Reckon Baldy'll make Prescott come the end of the week,' he said. 'Travels too slow, or you could send Storm MacKenzie a letter.'

Fanny looked mystified. Dave chuckled. 'Baldy passes the Diamond M ranch-house purty close . . . comes within two or three miles of where Stormy lives.' He went back more directly to the problem confronting the girl. 'Don't know when Stormy'll be in town again. Said he'd make it quick as he could.'

'He really should know.' Fanny was worried.

'It's in my mind to send word out to the ranch,' Dave went on. 'Reckon it's only right Stormy should know 'bout this mischief Ed's cookin' up with Yessap.' His look went to a man pitching straw down from a long rick that stood near the barn. 'Johnny,' he called. 'Go throw a saddle on the buckskin. Want you to ride out to the Diamond

M for me.' Dave paused. 'You can fetch that bay back, the one I loaned Stormy last evenin',' he added.

Relief was in the girl's smile. 'I hope you don't think I'm being silly about it, Mr. Stagg. I've told you exactly all that happened.'

'I've got the same notions about it that you have,' Dave assured her. He spoke soberly. 'Too bad Ed's been told you was up in the South Fork. I'd be kind of careful, if I was you, Miss Winston.'

The unmistakable warning note in his voice made Fanny look at him hard. He was telling her to beware of Ed Manners. She had unwittingly acquired a secret, and it was a dangerous one.

'I'll be careful, Mr. Stagg,' she promised. Her voice was not quite steady. 'I think I'll take my Baldy horse and go for a little ride.' She forced a light laugh. 'Your friend, Baldy Simpson, may have a mule he calls "Fanny," but he hasn't the best of me. I've a horse named "Baldy," and I can use my spurs on him if he's mean and tries to buck.'

Mr. Stagg chuckled, led the way into the long barn.

12
'The Winston Gal'

THE trail wound between low wooded slopes, followed the devious course of a brawling stream that dropped down from the higher hills. There was an exhilarating tang of spruce and pine in the air.

Fanny let her several problems go by the board. The sky was too blue, the morning too perfect. The dark mantle of doubts and fears was not to be worn on such a day.

She let the gray horse make his own pace, allowed herself to revel in each changing scene brought by the turn of the trail. It was a bewildering serpentine trail that repeatedly crossed the stream when the shallows permitted. She enjoyed the way Baldy leisurely splashed through the shallows, pausing occasionally to snuffle a mouthful of water between bridle-bits.

Dave Stagg had talked a lot about the Diamond M Ranch. Dave bought most of his horses from the Diamond M. Best horses in the Territory. Storm MacKenzie was that way, wouldn't stand for poor stuff on his ranch. Diamond M steers couldn't be beat for the prime beef they carried. Always brought top prices. Stormy was a smart cowman. Learned all a man could know about cows from his dad, and it was Dave's notion that old Jim MacKenzie had been weaned on a longhorn. What Jim didn't know about cows when he was boss of the Diamond M a feller could put in his eye. Jim MacKenzie had come into the Territory with a bunch of Texas longhorns that the years had developed into the best herd of white-faced Herefords on any man's range. Jim was always one to look ahead, was one of the first to cross his longhorn cows with good Hereford bulls. Stormy was like his dad, always one jump ahead of other folks with smart ideas for the good of the cattle country.

Fanny was not certain she understood all the things Dave Stagg told her. Some of his talk seemed a bit biological, but she felt an odd satisfaction in knowing that Storm MacKenzie was held in such high esteem. Not that he meant anything to her. She hardly knew him.

The girl's smooth brow puckered in a tiny frown. She was always thinking of Storm MacKenzie. It wouldn't do. She'd have to stop it. She was being absurd, allowing her thoughts to dwell on a man who probably didn't even know her name. Storm MacKenzie had only seen her once to speak to, those few moments in Mesalta when he had helped her with the Indian woman.

Fanny glanced at the silver-and-turquoise bracelet that clasped her arm. It was sweet of the shy little Navajo woman to give it to her. Some day soon she would look Maria up, take some gifts for her and the baby.

Baldy's head was suddenly high, she noticed, his ears twitching nervously. The same trick of his that had given her the timely warning in the South Fork.

Misgivings seized her. Her head went round in a quick look down the trail. A lone horseman! And riding fast.

Fanny's heart turned over and she took another look at the approaching rider. She couldn't be sure—not at that distance—but she had the impression the man wore a dark beard. Yes, she was positive, the rider was a bearded man. She caught the glint of sunlight on the rifle in saddle-boot.

With an effort she fought at a rising tide of panic. No chance, now, to return down the trail. The man might be Vordal. She couldn't afford the risk. She was seeing again that strange look in Ed Manners's eyes as he turned away into the barber shop. If the approaching rider was Vordal there could be only one answer. Manners had sent the man after her, must have been secretly watching her when she rode away from the livery barn.

She touched the gray horse with her spurs. Baldy broke into a fast gallop toward the cliff-girded portal of the upper canyon. Dave's voice was in the girl's ears as she rode. *I'd be kind of careful, if I was you.* Not careful enough, Fanny reflected bitterly. But who would dream Ed Manners would act so quickly! Dave Stagg said he was a rattlesnake, but a rattlesnake gave warning. This man struck without any warning.

The canyon was narrow, squeezed in between lofty cliffs, but the trail ran straight, followed the bed of the stream for almost a mile before twisting up in a corkscrew ascent. Fanny's eyes searched the cliffs for some sign of an opening in which she might hide. Nothing met her anxious gaze, only bare, unbroken sheer walls.

The gray was fast and strong—and sure-footed. He was a Diamond M horse, born and bred on Storm MacKenzie's ranch. Fanny found satisfaction, comfort, in the thought. She had a good start on her pursuer. His horse wouldn't be as fast as her speedy Baldy.

A quick glance over her shoulder told her the man was already inside the canyon. No doubting his intentions now. His horse was on the dead run.

Her heart skipped a beat. He was gaining on her. The going was more level near the mouth of the canyon and the gray horse was being slowed down by the sudden steep pitch as the trail went up the hairpin turns. It was not possible to move much faster than a shuffling running-walk. Fanny prayed for the first bend that would shut her from view. She dreaded a possible bullet from the man's rifle. She was sure he would not hesitate to shoot. Manners had sent him after her for only one purpose. She had chanced to learn his secret, a secret that might destroy him. He was determined to destroy her first, close her mouth forever.

She kept the gray horse moving as fast as safety permitted. The hairpin turns seemed endless. Fanny was thankful for them. They kept her pursuer from more than an occasional glimpse of her. She caught sight of him several times on the looping trail below. He was losing ground. His horse lacked Baldy's speed and stamina for the grueling ascent.

Suddenly they were on the barren summit of the ridge. Below her reached wave upon wave of other ridges, and, far beyond, the misty blue and mauve of the Painted Desert.

It was a view that would have enthralled her at any other moment. But what gladdened the girl's eyes most was the road ribboning through the wooded slopes below. Something moved down there, a crawling black dot—a lone horseman.

Fanny shook up the reins, sent the gray horse recklessly down the trail. That lone rider would be Johnny—the man Dave Stagg was sending with the message to Storm MacKenzie at the ranch. She had heard Johnny say he would take the long road to the ranch. Johnny was not liking the hard ride by way of the Juniper Flats shortcut.

Something else caught her straining eyes as Baldy scrambled and jumped and single-footed his way along the twisting, precipitous descent. Slow-moving wagons—Baldy Simpson's freight wagons, crawling behind a long black line of plodding mules. Dust lifted in a trailing dun plume.

Fanny was sure she would be safe if she could reach Johnny before Vordal overtook her. She was equally sure that only some mishap would give the man a chance to overhaul her faster horse.

Johnny heard her frantic call. He pulled his horse to a standstill, sat there in his saddle, wonder in his eyes as she came plunging down the hillside into the road. He was a skinny, elderly man with a stubble of gray beard on his chin.

'I'm being followed,' Fanny told him breathlessly. 'I'm frightened.'

'You're the Winston gal,' Johnny said in a surprised voice. His jaws worked agitatedly on tobacco quid. 'I don't carry no gun,' he added.

'I think he intends to kill me.' Fanny was surprised at the steadiness of her voice, a bit aghast at the stark horror of the simple statement.

'Don't carry no gun,' repeated Johnny. The Adam's apple in his long stringy neck moved convulsively.

'He's coming now.' Fanny's tone was frantic. 'Can't you do something?'

Vordal was partway down the last steep slope and coming at a reckless pace. The livery stable roustabout gave him a quick look. His pale blue eyes took on a hard gleam.

'You git out of here,' he said to the girl. 'I'll hold the cuss long enough for you to git a good start on him.'

Fanny nodded, gave Baldy his head, went pounding down the long grade. She glanced back at the turn, in time to see Johnny make a flying tackle from his saddle as Vordal's horse slid down the bank to the road. It gave her a choky feeling. Johnny wore no gun, but there was courage, fine courage. The scrawny little roustabout was a gallant knight in shining armor with only his courage to arm him.

The sound of a gunshot touched her ears, shocked her to the marrow. Johnny's laconic statement lashed at her. *Don't carry no gun.* Tears filled the girl's eyes. Johnny's courage was not enough. Johnny had no gun. Anger seized her, a white-hot rage against the man with the black beard. She tried to pull Baldy to a halt. She was not going to desert Johnny.

The gray horse was suddenly unmanageable. Perhaps the gunshot awoke disturbing memories. The bit was hard between his teeth and he went plunging away from the road, down the steep slope. A narrow chasm yawned in front of them, the deep wash of some ravaging cloudburst. Baldy rose into the air in a mighty jump that cleared the chasm and came down with a jolt that rocked Fanny crazily in her saddle. The next moment she was lying on the ground.

Fortunately, a clump of tough brush broke the fall, rolled her over sideways. She got to her feet, shaken, but unhurt, save a reddening scratch on the back of her hand. The gray horse had disappeared. Only the sound of his hammering hoofs fading in the distance.

She felt horribly afraid. Johnny dead, her horse gone, and somewhere near by, a man seeking her life.

Fanny began to run through the growth of scrubby trees. She had no idea of direction. Her sole thought was flight from the man Ed Manners had sent to kill her. Suddenly she was looking down at the road again. It must have made a wide loop, like an S lying on its side.

Dust hung in the air. She caught a glimpse of a high-wheeled wagon swinging around the bend some fifty yards away. Baldy Simpson's freight outfit on the long haul to Prescott.

Fanny was running even as she planned, remnants of her long riding skirt hiked high over one arm. Her driving urge was to overtake those disappearing wagons. They offered a haven, a hiding place Vordal would not suspect.

She caught up with the rear wagon, its high sides covered with securely roped tarpaulins. Fanny clutched at the endgate, let the slow-moving wagon pull her along for a few yards. She was out of breath, almost done for.

A corner of the tarpaulin was hanging loose. She glimpsed a blanket roll, and other miscellaneous articles, a lantern, horse-collars, halters, ropes—a toolbox. It was obvious Baldy Simpson used the end of his rear wagon as a carry-all.

Fanny was suddenly aware of a new sound that rose sharply above the rumble of the big wheels. The hammering of hoofs drawing up behind her. Vordal! Riding furiously—almost within reach of the bend around which she had just pursued the wagons.

The brief respite while the wagon pulled her along had given her a chance to recover her breath.

She ducked under the loose end of the tarpaulin and scrambled inside. It was a hard, muscle-straining operation. The wagon-bed was high, almost up to her shoulders, and the riding skirt hampered her unmercifully. But somehow she managed it, crouched down behind the blanket roll and tucked the trailing skirt around her legs.

It made a dark and smelly hiding place, but at that moment Fanny would not have traded it for all the vast open spaces of Arizona. She lay there, heedless of the smells, the jolting wheels, the blackness, and suddenly she heard the approaching rush of galloping hoofs, heard the rider's harsh voice hailing Baldy Simpson.

'No. Ain't seen no female ridin' a gray horse'— the freighter's quiet, curt voice. 'Ain't nobody passed me recent.'

'Sure is queer whar-all she got to,' grumbled the black-bearded rider. 'Seed her plain back yonder in the upper loop. Wasn't more'n fifteen minutes ago.' His voice trailed away in a string of oaths.

'You act like you're some upset, mister.' Baldy Simpson's tone was mildly curious. He had made no attempt to halt his team. 'Your old lady run out on you, or somethin'?'

'Naw. This here gal lives with her ma over in Dutch Flats. Went clean out of her haid. Crazy as a loon. We been lookin' all over for her.'

There was an expression of sympathy from the freighter, then: 'Reckon she must have headed some place else, mister. I'd have seen her if she rode this way.'

Fanny's straining ears caught a disappointed oath from Vordal, and suddenly he was riding back up the grade. She peeped cautiously, saw him disappear around the bend.

The great wagons rumbled and swayed their way down the grade, heavy brake-blocks screeching when the pitch steepened. Fanny relaxed on the blanket roll. She hadn't the least idea what to do, save remain where she was. No doubt, when evening came, Baldy Simpson would pull up at some wayside feed corral for the night. Time enough then to reveal herself. There would be other people at the wayside station. The thought brought Fanny some comfort. She did not want to face Baldy Simpson alone. For all she knew, the freighter might have swallowed Vordal's story about the crazy girl. No telling what he would do.

The high wheels churned on, the huge wagon groaned and swayed. Fanny bounced miserably on the bed roll. She wondered if she could possibly bear it, huddled under the dark stuffiness of the smelly tarpaulin. She wondered, too, what her mother would do when night came, and no Fanny. And what would Lester Warde do? Lester would rush to his friend and business crony, Ed Manners, with an appeal for help to find her. Ed Manners would be very smooth about it, express much concern, organize a hunt that would lead to nowhere.

Her failure to return to the hotel could mean only one thing to Ed Manners. She was dead, lying somewhere in the brush. His mind would be at rest, his secret safe.

Strange little sounds suddenly caught her attention, brought her aching head up from the bed roll. Odd little noises they were, like multitudinous fingers tapping on the tarpaulin above her.

She listened, startled, wide-eyed, and suddenly she understood. Rain! It was raining. She sank back against the bed roll, relieved, inclined to be amused at her momentary fright. She sat up again, listened tensely. The wagon wheels had stopped their grinding. All was suddenly quiet, a stillness broken only by the rapid beating of her heart. Something was about to happen. The wagons were no longer moving.

Her straining ears caught the sound of footsteps. Baldy Simpson had climbed down from his wheel horse, was approaching the rear wagon.

Fanny sat very still, incapable of movement. The footsteps came nearer, paused a time or two as if Baldy were examining his tie-ropes or observing the condition of the protecting tarpaulins. He was humming tunelessly, something about a girl named Susannah, and Baldy didn't want her to cry for him and he was off to Californy with a banjo on his knee.

For some reason, Fanny was aware of a vast relief. A suspicious man wouldn't be humming a thing like that. There was something reassuring in the homely sentiment. She needn't be afraid of Baldy Simpson.

A big hand grasped the loose end of the tarpaulin and pulled it wide open. Fanny found herself staring into the most amazed face she had ever seen.

The freighter let out a startled grunt. He gazed at her for a long moment, hand holding back the tarpaulin.

'Reckon you're the crazy gal that feller was lookin' for up the road a spell back,' he finally said.

Fanny shook her head. 'He wanted to kill me.' The simple statement came from her faintly.

'Huh?' Baldy Simpson stared incredulously. 'Kill you?' He wrinkled his brows. 'Sounds kind o' like crazy talk, you sayin' that.'

She spoke more loudly, angrily. 'I tell you that man would have killed me—if I hadn't hidden in this wagon. I heard him talking to you, telling you a silly story about a crazy girl.'

The freighter continued to stare at her, heedless of the increasing rain that beat down on his face. Tiny rivulets of water began to drip from his wide-brimmed hat. A puzzled look crept into his eyes, a glimmer of recognition. 'Say—ain't I seen you before some place?'

Fanny knew that she had won. She smiled faintly. 'Yes, Mr. Baldy Simpson. You were pulling out from the corral in Mesalta when I was talking to Dave Stagg. He told me who you were.'

Mr. Simpson muttered something under his breath. What he said had a profane tang to it. Fanny didn't mind. Her spirits had been below zero and now they were soaring. Nothing mattered, now she had found a friend.

'I'm afraid you're getting awfully wet,' she said a bit hysterically.

'I was back here to git my slicker,' explained the freighter.

'And found a surprise package instead.' She was getting hold of herself again, able to keep her voice steady.

The freighter chuckled. 'Could have knocked me down with a feather. Ain't never seen the like of it.' His leathery face hardened. 'Was wantin' to kill you, huh. Wish I'd a knowed his game when he come ridin' 'longside me the way he did.'

'I want to get down from this wagon,' interrupted the girl. 'I can't stand it here any longer. I'm so stiff I'm petrified.'

Baldy helped her down, reached inside the wagon for his slicker and threw it over her.

'I'm quite in a daze,' Fanny told him ruefully. 'I don't know what to do. I can't ride on and on with you.'

'Sure got me buffaloed, what to do,' admitted Baldy. He shook his head worriedly.

'Dave Stagg said you passed close to the Diamond M Ranch.' Fanny spoke hopefully. 'Are we near the ranch yet, Mr. Simpson?'

'Come within two or three miles of the Diamond M, but won't be that close till noon tomorrow.' The freighter's tone was regretful. 'You're knowin' Stormy MacKenzie?'

'Yes,' she answered simply. 'I've got to get to his place. It—it may mean life—or death—to him.' She was surprised at the tremble in her voice.

Baldy Simpson seemed not to be listening. His face was turned away, his gaze fixed down the road in the direction the wagons were headed. Fanny now caught the sound. Horsemen, two of them, showing vaguely through the driving rain.

The girl uttered a dismayed little cry, turned frantically to the wagon. Baldy's voice stopped her.

'MacKenzie,' he said in a relieved voice. 'Another feller with him. Reckon they run across your horse and have come lookin' for you.'

Surprise, and relief, held the girl speechless. She stood there, shivering with excitement and cold under the freighter's dripping slicker as she watched the approaching riders.

13
A Message Is Delivered

JOHNNY'S horse was nibbling at the grass in a little gully that ran down to the road. The animal's head lifted in an inquiring look at the approaching riders.

'Is this the place?' Storm's glance went to the girl.

Fanny nodded. 'I remember the gully,' she replied. 'Johnny turned up here when he heard me calling to him.'

'Señor'—Miguel was pointing—'I see heem—over there in those broosh.'

'Wait here,' Storm said to Fanny. He rode up the road a few yards. The Mexican followed him and the watching girl saw them get down from their saddles and bend over something lying there in a clump of greasewood. She averted her eyes.

'He ees mooch dead,' Miguel muttered. His brown eyes took on a glassy hardness as he stared down at the murdered stable-hand.

'He was a brave man,' Storm said.

'He no 'ave gun.' Miguel shook a disapproving head. '*Por Dios!* I theenk eet wise 'ave gun all time. Me—I wear gun all time.' He patted the butt of the forty-five in his holster.

'Johnny wasn't looking for trouble,' Storm reminded. He shifted his gaze to the browsing horse. 'We'll have to get the body back to town, Miguel.'

The wrangler nodded, swung his horse and rode away. In less than five minutes he was back with the dead man's animal.

Storm lifted the slain roustabout in his arms. 'Get your rope, Miguel.'

They lashed the body across the saddle. The Mexican's face had a grayish look. He was not caring for this business.

'All right, Miguel. You bring him along. Don't follow us too closely. It is not good for the señorita to see this thing.'

Miguel took the lead-rope. *'Si,'* he muttered. 'I will remember, señor.'

He waited there on his horse while Storm returned to the girl.

'We're taking Johnny back to town,' he told her. 'Miguel will follow us with the body.'

She gave him an aghast look. 'I'm afraid,' she said quickly. 'I'm afraid to go back to that place.'

'I'll be with you—'

The rain had slackened to a light drizzle. Far down the road they could see Baldy Simpson's freight wagons topping a rise. Storm's slicker had replaced the one Baldy had loaned Fanny. It hung wet and glistening about her slender form, kept out the chill wind, but could not keep the chill from her heart.

'You must not make me go back,' she said in a low voice. 'I won't be safe in that town.'

Storm's look went to the waiting Miguel, came back to the girl. 'You haven't told me just what the trouble is,' he said. 'Only that some man followed you, and that Johnny got shot trying to stop him.'

'I'm not going back to that town,' she said again.

'All right.' Storm spoke soothingly. 'I'll take you to the ranch.' He swung his horse and rode back to the Mexican youth.

Fanny waited, not looking. She could not bear to

look at that dead man tied to the saddle of the led horse. She heard Storm's quiet voice, the Mexican's reply, and presently, Storm was back at her side.

'Let's go,' he said.

They rode away, down the road. Fanny's ears caught the sounds of clattering hoofs as Miguel moved off in the opposite direction with Johnny's horse at the end of a lead-rope.

Storm showed no impatience to hear her story. He sensed her frayed nerves. He'd been helping Miguel round up some colts, he told her. The gray horse had suddenly galloped up.

'I was thrown off when Baldy jumped a little gully,' confessed Fanny.

'I knew he was from Dave's stable,' Storm said. 'I sold that horse to Dave.'

'Baldy was heading straight back to the home ranch.' Fanny's tone was rueful. 'If only I could have stuck to the saddle.'

'You wanted to come to the ranch?'

'Not at—at first'—Fanny's voice was unsteady again. 'I—I had to get to the ranch—after what happened to Johnny.'

She found herself telling him everything, the chance encounter with Red Yessap and Manners in the South Fork. Storm listened without comment.

'Dave Stagg warned me to be careful,' finished the girl. 'He said that Manners might be more dangerous than a rattlesnake.'

'Manners guessed that you had seen him with

Red Yessap,' Storm said. 'He didn't know how much you might have overheard.'

'He should be arrested,' declared Fanny.

Storm shook his head. 'The sheriff is afraid of Ed Manners. He'd claim your story was crazy. He wouldn't take your word against Manners.'

'Vordal can be arrested,' argued the girl. 'Vordal shot Johnny.'

'Manners would deny any connection with Vordal,' Storm pointed out. 'Getting Vordal wouldn't remove the danger, and you can be sure that Vordal will go into hiding.'

They had left the road and were following a trail that wound over a ridge. The drizzle of rain had stopped and sunshine lay in the long valley below them. Fanny glimpsed the silvery thread of a creek and low ranch buildings set in a great grove of trees. She reined the gray horse to a standstill.

'Is that the ranch?'

'The Diamond M,' Storm told her.

'I like it,' she said simply.

'I was born in that house.'

'I like it,' the girl said again. 'It looks so—so peaceful—so safe.' She straightened up in the saddle with a dismayed exclamation. 'I should have sent some word to Mother by that Mexican. I don't want her to worry.'

'I told Miguel to have Dave tell her you'll be at the ranch,' Storm said.

Fanny gave him a grateful look, and then, worriedly: 'She won't know what to think. She'll wonder if I'm crazy.'

'I'm only hoping she won't tell Ed Manners.' Storm shook his head. 'Seems best for her to know where you are, or she'd be having the hills searched.'

'Mother is sure to tell Lester Warde,' Fanny admitted ruefully. 'And Lester will probably tell Mr. Manners. It's just too bad Mother had to know.'

'We'll have to let things work out,' Storm said with a shrug of his shoulders. 'You can't go back to town—not until things have been made safe.'

She gave him a sidewise glance. 'I'm wondering just how things will be made safe. What can one do?'

Storm made no answer, and the girl, looking at him, saw that his eyes were very grim.

Presently he smiled round at her. 'Ynes is going to be surprised,' he said.

'Who is Ynes?' There was a hint of consternation in her answering look. It hadn't occurred to her that Storm MacKenzie might—might be *married*. 'You mean your wife?'

Storm's smile broadened. 'Ynes is boss of the ranch-house, but she isn't my wife. She's been with the Diamond M since before I was born. You'll like her,' he added soberly.

Storm found himself wondering what Ynes would say when she saw the girl he was so strangely bringing home to the old ranch-house.

145

14
War Dance Trail

THE steers Jim Race had combed out of the cedar brakes were doing well up in Wild Horse Flats. The grass was plentiful, and, as the foreman pointed out, they could fill their bellies without having to walk their fat off looking for something to get their tongues around.

'Beats me why they hanker to git back to their ol' stompin'-ground,' Jim grumbled. 'Give 'em a chance an' they head back for the brakes. Seems like cows is awful dumb.'

'They were born in the brakes,' Storm pointed out. 'They get homesick for their own country.'

'Well'—the foreman chuckled—'this bunch'll never see the brakes ag'in.' He lolled easily in his saddle, fingers shaping a cigarette. 'We can start the drive most any time, Stormy. Close to three hundred head here in the flats. We can figger on two hundred more down on the Little Mesalta. High Hat sent word he can start 'em for Red Canyon Corral any time.'

'No hurry,' Storm said. 'Burl Jenners doesn't want delivery yet.'

'Grass enough here to keep 'em in good shape,' commented the foreman. 'Ain't worryin' about the *grass*.'

Storm gave him a shrewd look. 'What's getting you gloomy all of a sudden?'

'Ain't gloomy,' denied Jim. 'Just thinkin'.'

'Well—what's on your mind?'

'Rustlers,' Jim Race answered. 'No chance for the cows to git away from here unless rustlers pull off a raid when we ain't lookin' for trouble.'

'It's up to you, Jim. It's your job to see that rustlers don't get the jump on us.'

'That's what gits me worried,' grumbled the foreman. 'Sure will be glad to turn this bunch o' beef over to Jenners. Won't be sleepin' good for worryin' about what Red Yessap'll be figgerin' to spring on us.'

'Don't blame you.' Storm spoke grimly. 'I've an idea Yessap will try some trick on us, Jim. That's why we're up in the flats this morning. Want to look things over with you.'

'Figgered somethin' was on your mind,' commented the foreman. He glowered at his cigarette. 'Sure was a crime—Yessap gittin' loose from Yuma. He's a wolf—with the cunnin' of a coyote.'

'We've got to be smarter,' Storm said.

'Smartest thing we can do is lay for him with a dose o' lead poison.' Jim's craggy face crinkled in a hard smile. 'I crave to git him lined up in front of my rifle.'

'Getting Yessap is only part of the job,' Storm told the foreman.

'Huh?' Jim's tone was startled. 'You think there's some feller backin' up Red in this rustlin'?'

'It looks that way to me,' answered Storm. 'Pete

Kendall of the Lazy K is sure there's somebody with brains working with Yessap.'

'Huh.' Jim's tone was thoughtful. 'Meanin' you've spotted a king wolf layin' back in the brush some place.' His eyes narrowed in a searching stare at his boss. 'You've got me guessin', Stormy.'

'It's guesswork right now, Jim. Something like a puzzle picture, with the pieces scattered all over the place.'

'We've got to put 'em together,' muttered the foreman. 'Make them pieces talk sense.'

Storm's gaze was fixed on the sawtooth ridge that flanked the east slope. 'Maybe we can pick up some pieces up there that will help give us a start on the job.'

'Up on the old War Dance, huh?' Jim squinted his eyes in a long look. 'What gives you the notion we can pick up sign on the War Dance?'

The two men swung across the flats, were soon cautiously working their way up the steep, boulder-strewn slope. It was slow going. Presently Storm slid from his saddle.

'We'll have to do some scrambling, Jim.'

'We could make the climb better if we was cats,' grumbled the foreman.

They made no attempt to put the horses on lead-ropes. Storm knew Cacique would follow, and Jim's horse would not want to be left alone.

Another half-mile brought them to the crest of

the ridge. Jim Race made no bones about the way he felt. He sank down, breathless, on a flat boulder.

'I ain't what I used to be,' he confessed. 'Kind o' wore me down, scalin' them rocks. Mebbe good exercise for lizards, but is sure almighty tough on a cowboy.'

'You're getting soft, Jim,' bantered the younger man.

The foreman was unabashed. 'Only got one pair o' legs,' he retorted. 'Don't figger to compete none with centipedes an' such. Well—reckon yonder's the War Dance.'

There was little left of the trail made by generations of Apaches. Less experienced eyes would have passed it by or mistaken it for an animal trail. Storm knew better. The signs were plain that men had once passed this way, in fact quite recently. He picked up a piece of flinty rock, showed it to his companion.

The chip was fresh, made within the week by the shod hoof of a horse. No wandering cow had left that scar on the piece of rock in Storm's hand.

'What do you think?' Storm spoke softly.

'Same as you.' Jim got to his feet, jerked his gun from holster and carefully examined it. 'I'm thinkin' we'd best keep our eyes peeled,' he said grimly. 'No tellin' what we'll run into.'

Storm tossed the piece of rock away and turned to his horse. His thoughts were on Fanny Winston's story of the scene in the South Fork. He was grateful to the girl for the timely warning. He divined it was somewhere up in the War Dance Hills overlooking Red Canyon Corral that he would find the answer to the mysterious meeting between Ed Manners and Red Yessap.

Jim Race was looking at him curiously. He was not one to ask questions. Storm would tell him when he was ready. Jim knew how it was with Stormy. He liked to work things out in his mind. The foreman, watching the trail with wary eyes, finally ventured a remark.

'Looks like more'n one feller's been usin' the trail recent,' he said.

'Three riders, I make it,' Storm agreed.

'Wonder what their game is.' Jim shook his head. 'Ain't none of our boys come up here on the War Dance in a month o' Sundays. Would have heard about it.'

'We can make a pretty good guess,' Storm said grimly.

'Red Yessap, huh?'

'You've said it.' Storm gave the foreman a brief account of Fanny Winston's story.

'Always did size up Manners for a crook.' The foreman squinted a sidewise glance at Storm. 'Was wonderin' how come you got the girl stayin' at the ranch.'

'Her life is in danger, Jim. No question but what Vordal was sent to get her. I'm not letting her go back to town until this thing is settled.'

Jim's face wore a grim look. 'I don't put it past Manners to try an' shut her mouth,' he said. 'She knows too much.'

Suddenly they were looking down into the bowl of Red Canyon Corral, nestled under the rising tiers of jagged pinnacles.

For a long moment they stared, wordless, each man busy with his own thoughts. Jim Race finally said softly: 'Wouldn't be here. Could be seen easy, up here.'

They rode another quarter of a mile, following the encircling cliffs, and halted near a growth of piñon trees. There were signs there that made the two men exchange significant looks. They climbed from their saddles.

Storm came to a standstill, stared at something lying in the sparse short grass.

'Cigarette stub,' he said.

'Plenty of 'em layin' 'round,' commenced Jim Race. 'Reckon one of the fellers stayed here with the horses.'

'Let's see where the others went.' Storm was scrutinizing the faint tracks. They led to the edge of the rimrock, telltale imprints of booted feet. Jim Race muttered profane words as he followed the younger man. Unpleasant pictures were shaping in his mind, pictures that made his hair stand on end.

'I've been awful dumb,' he grumbled. 'Should have been more careful. A few fellers hid out here on the War Dance could have played hell with us down in the stone corral.'

There was no answer from Storm. His silence was like the bite of a spur in the foreman's ribs. He grunted, gave Storm a shamefaced look. 'Why don't you say what's in your mind?' Jim stared at the telltale cigarette butts that littered the ground close to a mass of tumbled red boulders. 'Why don't you bawl me out for a doggone fool?'

Storm turned and looked at him. 'I'm saying somebody's a fool, Jim, only it's not *you* I'm blaming.' Storm's tone was bitter. 'I'm the fool. It was up to me to think about the possibilities up here on War Dance.'

Jim Race glared at him. 'You're like your dad, Stormy. Won't let nobody take blame for nothin'.'

'I'm the boss of the Diamond M,' rejoined Storm. 'Makes me sick to think of what might have happened because of my carelessness.' He stared gloomily across the cascading pinnacles down into the bowl. 'We've used the stone corral so long it never occurred to me—this set-up here.'

'Makes my hair curl,' muttered the foreman. 'We wouldn't have a chance, down there.' He shook his head, unwittingly echoed Red Yessap's remark to Vordal. 'Easy as pottin' rabbits.'

Storm was staring across at the opposite cliffs. The set-up was perfect. Not a man of the Diamond M outfit could have escaped.

Fragments of Fanny Winston's tale of the

meeting in the South Fork came back to him. *The stone corral . . . War Dance . . . Storm MacKenzie . . . somebody was going to fix Storm MacKenzie.* The whole thing sounded crazy. Storm knew it wasn't crazy. Spies had been watching the Diamond M men at work in the stone corral below.

Jim Race was muttering to himself. Storm caught the words. *Would have played hell with the Jenners shipment.* A sudden light flared within Storm, a bright, illuminating flash of memory. His talk with Ed Manners that night after his deal with the cattle-buyer.

Storm recalled the conversation with some dismay. He had revealed the full details of the Jenners deal to Ed Manners. He began to understand Manners's insistence about the quitclaim deed that would give him possession of the Palos Verdes slopes if the note was not repaid when due. Manners did not want the note repaid and had plotted with Red Yessap to steal the steers.

There were angles that puzzled Storm. Manners had loaned him the money to buy the Palos Verdes slopes from Hendricks. Non-payment of the note would make Manners the actual purchaser of the property. Storm couldn't make sense out of it. Manners's only chance for a profit would be a resale to Lester Warde for a much higher figure.

Jim Race said in his slow, patient voice, 'Got the thing figgered out, Stormy?'

Storm shook his head gloomily. 'It's too deep for me, Jim.'

'We're a jump ahead of 'em at that, Stormy.' Grim satisfaction put a rasp in the foreman's voice. 'We'll be ready for them wolves when they lay for us up on War Dance.'

Storm looked at him. He was remembering the attempt to kill Fanny Winston because she had chanced upon a dangerous secret. He said bitterly: 'I'm hoping Vordal will be there. We'll leave him on War Dance for the buzzards.'

15
The Pot Begins to Boil

THREE passengers climbed down from Al Penner's stage. One of them was Burl Jenners, the portly Kansas City cattle-buyer. Judging from the gravity of his expression and the rather grim look he gave Ed Manners as the latter strolled over from his bank, there was much on his mind to worry Mr. Jenners. With an unsmiling nod for Al he started across the street toward the Stagg House.

The man who followed him down from the dusty coach was Lester Warde, clad in a long and crumpled linen coat. Ed Manners beckoned him.

'Got bad news for you Les—'

'Save it,' growled Warde. His look went longingly to the swing doors of the Palace Bar. 'I'm needing a cool drink. Been eating dust all the way from Flagstaff.'

'Your girl's run off,' Manners told him.

Warde halted in his stride. 'You're crazy.' His face reddened and with an angry gesture he pushed through the swing doors.

Manners followed him. 'I'm giving it to you straight.' He led the way to a corner table. 'Let's sit over here where we can talk. It's serious business, Les.'

Al Penner's third passenger wore the high-heeled boots of a cowman. He moved with short, choppy strides across the dusty street, went clattering along the board sidewalk toward Dave Stagg's livery barn. Dave, tilted back in his ancient wooden chair in front of his office door, looked up from the plug of tobacco he was shaving into his hand.

'Howdy, Pete. Just off the stage, huh?'

'Come in from Holbrook by way of Flagstaff,' Kendall told him. 'Busted a wheel an' had to leave the buckboard in Flagstaff. Caught Al Penner just as he was pullin' out for Mesalta.'

'Must have been in a hurry to git here,' commented Dave. He began tamping the tobacco into the charred bowl of his pipe.

The Holbrook rancher's always belligerent red face looked more angry than ever. His smallish red-rimmed eyes had the furious glare of an incensed bull.

'Guess you know what brings me back to Mesalta so soon, Dave.' Kendall's tone was bitter. 'I ain't restin' till I catch the skunk that killed my line-rider. Never was one to sit twiddlin' my thumbs when there's a murderin' killer like Red Yessap prowlin' loose in the brush.'

Dave put a match to his pipe. There was a drawn look to his face. 'Some feller got Johnny a night or two back.' Dave drew hard on the pipe. 'Stormy's Mexican wrangler found him layin' in the brush—fetched him in.'

'Johnny?' Kendall lifted bristly eyebrows in a glance at the corrals.

'Yeah—him. . . . Wasn't good for much, been kind of ailin' with his stummick . . . only give him the light work 'round the barn, pitchin' straw for the stalls an' rubbin' up harness an' saddle gear.'

'How come Johnny got shot?' Kendall shook his head sorrowfully. 'Mighty sorry about him, Dave.'

'Sent him over to the Diamond M with a letter for Stormy—'

The Holbrook cattleman interrupted him. 'Guess it's plain enough, Dave—' he spoke wrathfully. 'Somethin' to do with Red Yessap, huh? An' Red Yessap got wise, was layin' for Johnny.'

'No, Pete'—Dave shook his head. 'You're on the wrong trail, figgerin' 'twas Yessap.' Dave paused, puffed vigorously on his pipe. 'Ain't claimin' Yessap wasn't mixed up in the killin' someways.'

'Sure he was,' declared Kendall angrily. 'You an' me know Yessap's gunnin' for Stormy. He must have got wind of this letter you was sendin' to the Diamond M.'

'Stormy's in a tight fix,' Dave said gloomily.

'Wish we was over in *my* county,' grumbled Kendall. 'We have a sheriff that ain't scared of his own shadder.'

'Vin Terrill's afraid of his mortgage,' Dave Stagg commented grimly.

'You should elect you a *real* sheriff,' fumed the Holbrook rancher. 'Storm MacKenzie should be sheriff in this county.'

'Got to elect him first,' reminded Dave. 'Manners is some politician . . . got an awful lot of votes corralled, what with all the lumberjacks in the Little Mesalta.'

'You're up against it plenty hard,' Kendall declared. 'Vin Terrill won't raise a hand. Manners owns him body and soul. He won't touch Yessap if Manners tells him to lay off.'

'Stormy'll figger out somethin',' asserted Dave Stagg. 'He's awful law-abidin' . . . thinks a heap o' the law an' havin' folks keep it.'

'He won't git much justice from the law in *this* county,' grumbled Kendall. 'Not while Manners has the law in his pocket.'

'You can push a man just so far,' observed Dave. 'I'm remindin' you that Stormy was never one to be pushed 'round easy.'

'I'd sure like to have a talk with him,' mused Kendall. 'Got a notion to head for his ranch right now, Dave.'

'Better wait till mornin',' counseled the liveryman. 'Shouldn't wonder but what Stormy may be in town. Sent him word to come soon as he could make it. Want to talk to him myself . . . figger out some way to git Ed Manners redhanded. Sure looks like he's in with Yessap an' we've got to prove it on him.'

The Holbrook man nodded. He wasn't keen on the long ride to the Diamond M. It would be dark before he arrived and no telling but what some sneaking drygulcher would take a shot at him.

'Yuma's stoppin' at the hotel,' Dave remarked.

Kendall said he knew that Yuma was in town. 'Told him to stick 'round . . . keep his eyes an' ears open.'

'Spends a heap o' time over at the Palace Bar,' Dave said with a chuckle.

'That's all right.' Kendall smiled grimly. 'Yuma's smart . . . got big ears.' The cattleman's look went to a buckboard rattling past. 'There's Vin Terrill.'

'Vin don't put up at my barn no more,' remarked Dave. His gaze followed the buckboard. 'Guess Ed told him to keep away from me.'

'Tyin' up in front of Ed's hotel,' muttered Kendall.

'Vin'll make for the bar quick as he can git

there,' chuckled Dave. 'Vin ain't happy unless he's got a pint of whiskey under his belt. Suits Ed Manners to keep him that way. Makes Vin easier to handle.'

Kendall grunted angrily. 'The low-down toad!' He turned away. 'Guess I'll git over to the Stagg House an' wash some of the dust off of me.'

'Burl Jenners come in on the stage with you.' Dave's tone was mildly curious. 'Was noticin' he looked kind o' hot under the collar.'

'Somethin' on Burl's mind,' Kendall said. 'Thought more'n once he was goin' to say what was worryin' him.'

'What stopped him?' Dave shook his head. 'Burl most always talks plenty—too much, once in a while.'

'Won't be certain I'm right, Dave'—the Holbrook man's tone was thoughtful. 'Seemed to me it was that Warde feller that stopped Burl from tellin' me what was on his mind. He'd start to speak, look over at Warde, settin' there in front, an' shut up tight as a clam.'

'Huh.' Dave pondered, brows drawn down in a perplexed frown. 'Warde's awful thick with Ed. Reckon that's the answer, Pete.'

Kendall nodded. 'I savvy. Burl wasn't wantin' Warde to hear . . . was afraid he'd tell Manners.'

'That's my notion of it,' agreed the liveryman. 'Well, *adios* for now, Pete. See you supper time.'

The cowman nodded, went with his short choppy

stride up the board sidewalk. Dave Stagg watched him, cold pipe clenched between his teeth, his face sober, thoughtful. The pot was beginning to boil, and the brew promised to be unpleasant.

16
A Warrant for Arrest

A MORE astute man than Lester Warde would have noticed a subtle change in Ed Manners. The general manager of the Great Western Land and Timber Company was not strong on psychology. He was better at estimating the board feet of lumber he could cut from a tall pine tree. The occasional hint of fear in Ed's eyes made no impression on Warde. If he thought anything at all about his friend's manifestations of taut nerves, he put it down to the mysterious behavior of Fanny Winston.

'The girl must be crazy!' Warde's big hand tightened over the whiskey bottle on the table. 'She's never met MacKenzie—far as I know.'

'You ain't a noticin' man, Les.' Ed Manners made no attempt to conceal his irritation. 'She was talkin' to him the afternoon Yessap took a shot at him in the street. Seemed kind of taken with him, too.'

Warde's face reddened angrily. 'First I've heard of it.'

'Proves she didn't want you to know,' sneered Manners.

'She's crazy,' repeated Warde sullenly. He could think of no other reason that would explain his friend's amazing story about the girl.

Ed Manners was watching him closely. Fanny's escape from Vordal promised unpleasant consequences. The girl had seen him with Red Yessap, probably had overheard their conversation. She would have told Storm MacKenzie the story by now. The thought made Ed inwardly writhe, appalled him. Vordal's failure to get the girl was likely to ruin him, put him behind the bars, or worse, place a noose around his neck. Strange, how the girl had managed to elude Vordal. The latter had returned with the belief the girl was lost in the brush. That was bad enough, but not hopeless. Still a chance to find her, shut her mouth in the only way possible. The hope was blasted by Dave Stagg's story carried to Mrs. Winston. The girl was at the MacKenzie ranch. She'd been thrown from her horse and somehow managed to find her way to the Diamond M.

Warde started to get out of his chair. 'I'm going after her—'

Manners stopped him. 'Don't go off half-cock. It's a job for Terrill. I sent for him. . . . He's the one to get the girl back.'

'The sheriff?' Warde relaxed into his chair. 'Don't need the sheriff,' he grumbled.

'He'll have Mrs. Winston swear out a warrant.' Ed paused, added significantly: 'No tellin' what shape the girl will be in, Les. Bad shock. She maybe won't be herself.'

Warde paled. 'It's hell,' he muttered. 'Makes me see red. She's crazy, or else MacKenzie's holding her against her will.'

'Some fond of her, ain't you, Les?'

'Was only waiting for her to set the day,' confided the lumberman.

'Like as not she'll be out of her head—talk wild—say crazy things.' Manners proceeded to hammer home the thought he wanted to fix in Warde's mind. Warde would not have a chance to talk to Fanny Winston if his plans worked out. If Warde did get to the girl it must be with the conviction in his mind that she was probably out of her head—that any wild accusations against Manners were the absurd ravings of a disordered brain. 'Just as well you don't see her until she's had a chance to get hold of herself,' he advised.

'It's my right to be with her,' muttered Warde. 'She needs me.'

'I'm tellin' you for your own good,' Manners said soothingly. 'You listen to me, Les. Keep out of this mess. Terrill will have the girl back in no time.'

'Mrs. Winston must be sick with worry. Guess I'll run over to the hotel, Ed. She'll want to know I'm back in town and ready to stand by.'

'Good idea,' agreed Manners. 'I'll bring Terrill over soon as he gits in town. Should be here most any minute.'

Warde got out of his chair. 'Thanks, Ed. Maybe you're right about letting Terrill handle it.'

'Sure I'm right,' asserted Manners. He made a sly attempt to divert the lumberman's mind. 'Things are shapin' up first class,' he said. 'I'll have MacKenzie in a tight hole. He won't be payin' off that note, Les. You'll be loggin' that Hendricks yellow pine inside of a month.'

'All I want right now is to get Fanny back.' Warde spoke angrily. 'The next thing I want is to throw MacKenzie in jail.'

'You leave it to Vin Terrill,' reassured Ed Manners. He gave the glowering Warde a crooked smile. 'You go cheer up Mrs. Winston. She's awful upset, been throwin' hysterics.'

Left alone at the corner table, Manners sat scowling at the whiskey bottle. Stark fear looked from his eyes. His big talk about the sheriff's getting the girl away from Storm MacKenzie was only for Warde's benefit. He was not at all confident Terrill would succeed, not with Storm MacKenzie at the ranch. Storm was a tough proposition. He'd throw Terrill off the place.

The swing doors pushed open. Manners looked up, saw Sheriff Vin Terrill making for the bar.

'Got a bottle over here, Vin,' he called out. 'Bring your glass with you.'

The sheriff approached and drew out a chair. 'Where's Johnnycake?' he wanted to know. 'Quit you?'

'Fired him,' grunted Manners.

Terrill showed interest. 'Johnnycake was a first-rate cook. Could use him over at the ranch.'

'No chance.' Manners spoke sourly. 'Johnnycake went back on the Diamond M payroll.' He tipped the bottle, filled the sheriff's glass. 'Got a job for you, Vin.'

'Yeah?' Terrill's tone was uneasy. He picked up the brimming glass with a suddenly shaky hand. 'I ain't your hired man, Ed.'

'Don't get your back up so quick. This is a job for the law.'

'Let's have the details.' Terrill put on a heavy frown befitting the high dignity of his office and reached for the bottle. 'Who do you want throwed into jail?'

'Storm MacKenzie.'

Sheriff Terrill's jaw dropped, instinctively his hand went out to the glass. Manners obligingly tipped the bottle.

'Thanks.' The sheriff downed the drink, shuddered, and drew shirtsleeve across damp mustache. 'Don't seem like Stormy would be turnin' crook.' He spoke dubiously. 'I'd say you was *loco*, Ed.'

'I'm doin' the thinkin' about this case, Vin. I ain't askin' what *you* think.'

Sheriff Terrill's sunburned face took on a mottled look. 'Sure, Ed. I wasn't sayin' you—'

'All you got to do is what I say,' interrupted

Manners. 'MacKenzie's run off with a girl who's been stayin' at the Palace with her ma. This girl is engaged to marry Les Warde. Don't savvy MacKenzie's game, but he went an' grabbed the girl when she was out ridin'. Her ma is havin' hysterics. She wants you to go fetch her back to town.'

It seemed a large order to the sheriff. Storm MacKenzie would likely pull a gun on him, he objected.

'You're the law,' Ed Manners pointed out. 'MacKenzie can't buck the law. All you got to do is to git Mrs. Winston to swear out a warrant.'

The prospect of confronting Storm MacKenzie on such an errand and on his own doorstep visibly daunted the sheriff. He sat slumped in his chair, stared with haggard eyes at the now empty bottle. Manners crooked a finger at the bartender, who promptly reached a fresh bottle from his shelf and brought it over. He took the occasion to whisper in the saloon man's ear.

'Ducker just come in. Wants to speak to you private.'

Ed nodded. 'Fill up your glass, Vin. Be back in a minute.' He followed the white-aproned drink-dispenser back to the bar. 'What you want with me, Ducker?'

Ducker, hairy hand fastened on his whiskey glass, looked round. 'Just seen MacKenzie ride up the street. He's over at Stagg's barn right now.'

Manners pondered a moment. 'Don't let him see

you, Ducker. He may have got a look at you the other night when you an' Vordal trailed him.'

The squat-faced man nodded, said he'd sneak out the back way and hole up in Frenchy Jack's place.

'Fine.' Manners's look went briefly to the sheriff. 'Tell Frenchy to bring a couple of fellers with him quick as he can make it.'

The old glitter was back in the saloon man's eyes when he returned to the corner table. 'Luck's with us, Vin. MacKenzie's in town. You won't have to run up ag'in him out at the ranch.'

The sheriff brightened. He drained his glass and got to his feet. 'Let's go git that warrant sworn to,' he said. The whiskey was giving him trouble with his tongue.

'Sure,' assented Manners. He paused on the way out and spoke to the bartender. The latter nodded.

'I'll tell Frenchy to wait here for you,' he promised.

Manners explained to the sheriff as they pushed out to the sidewalk. 'Soon as you've fixed up the warrant paper with Mrs. Winston you'll have to locate MacKenzie an' throw him in jail.'

Terrill gave him an aghast look. Manners smiled. 'I've sent for Frenchy Jack an' a couple of other fellers. You can swear 'em in as deputies. Won't be no trouble handlin' MacKenzie. His own fault if he gits killed resistin' arrest.'

Terrill drew a long breath. 'Damn you, Ed. I'm gettin' sick—doin' your dirty work.'

'You'll be a lot sicker if you ain't careful,' retorted Manners. His smile was unpleasantly significant.

The sheriff wilted. He was thinking of a mortgage long past due.

'Let's go git the warrant fixed up,' he said thickly.

'That's the stuff,' approved Manners. He led the way into the hotel lobby.

Mrs. Winston was in a bad way. She was completely unnerved by the dreadful thing that had happened, she told the sheriff. Yes, she was sure her daughter had been kidnapped. No other explanation was possible. She had seen that terrible man talking to Fanny. He must have fallen in love with her.

'I'm goin' after her quick as you sign this warrant paper,' the sheriff told her.

Mrs. Winston made a shaky signature. 'You'll go with him, won't you, Lester?' She looked at Warde tearfully.

The sheriff, already cued by Manners, shook his head. 'Don't want him along,' he said gruffly.

Warde looked rebellious. 'Fanny will want me,' he protested angrily.

'I'm runnin' this show.' Sheriff Terrill glared at him. 'I'm the law, an' what I says goes.' He smiled at the distracted mother. 'Don't you worry none, ma'am. I'll have deputies along with me. We'll take good care of the girl . . . bring her back safe an' sound to you.'

'You leave it to him, Mrs. Winston,' Manners reassured the widow. He looked at Warde. 'See you later, Les. Got some news for you.' He followed Terrill into the street, laid a hand on the sheriff's shoulder. 'Listen, Vin. These are orders. I'm sendin' French Jack along with you to see that you mind 'em.'

Terrill's face paled. 'What do you mean, Ed?' He gulped. 'Ain't likin' your tone.'

'When you git that girl you're takin' her over to your ranch an' keepin' her there. Savvy?'

'No,' muttered the sheriff. 'I don't savvy.'

'I don't want her back in this town,' Manners told him. 'I've got reasons.'

'What'll I do with her at the ranch?' Terrill showed fright.

'Just keep her at the ranch till I send word, or come out myself. Nothin' for you to worry about,' added Manners.

'Guess it's all right if you say so,' Terrill said unhappily. His gloomy look went across the street to the Stagg House. 'Guess I'll git those deputies sworn in an' go after MacKenzie.'

'Frenchy'll be in the bar now,' Ed Manners replied. There was an exultant gleam in his eyes as he led the way back to the saloon. He paused at the door, looked at his worried companion. 'She'll likely give you a lot of wild talk—about me. Don't take any stock in it, Vin. She's queer in the head, got notions.'

'Crazy, huh?' Terrill showed relief. 'I savvy. Ain't wantin' her ma to know, huh? Want to give the gal a chance to come out of it.'

'You've guessed it,' Manners said curtly.

'What'll her ma say when I don't bring her back?'

'Leave that to me.' Manners pushed through the door into the saloon. Sheriff Terrill followed. It was in his mind that he needed a long drink. He had a warrant for arrest in his pocket. The sheriff felt that something was very wrong. The job promised unpleasant possibilities.

17
Storm Baits a Trap

THE twilight was fading before the onrush of night when Storm and Jim rode out of an arroyo and turned into the Mesalta road. Lights began to glimmer faintly in the town. A sound broke through the stillness of eventide—the soft jangle of bells.

'Sarah Stagg's callin' Dave to supper,' Jim Race said. 'She always rings them old mule bells for him to come an' git it.' The foreman chuckled. 'Hope Sarah's got fresh apple pie tonight. Kind of hanker for fresh apple pie.'

'You've got a little job of work to do before you eat,' reminded Storm.

'Ain't forgettin',' Jim assured him.

'Don't need to get drunk doing it,' warned his boss good-naturedly.

'No call for me to git likkered,' Jim Race told him. 'Always plenty fellers quick to line up at the bar when the drinks is free. All I got to do is to talk noisy. If Ed Manners ain't there he'll hear the news I'll be spreadin'.' Jim's smile was grim. 'He'll git the news we want him to have about us fixin' to work cattle over in Red Canyon Corral tomorrow.'

'If we're right about him he's watching our movements,' Storm said.

'You bet we're right about him,' declared the foreman. 'The crawlin' snake!'

'Make sure you spread yourself in the saloon,' Storm instructed him. 'Tell him plenty, Jim.'

'Leave it to me, boss.' Jim chuckled. 'Ed's goin' to know we're shippin' those Jenners cows tomorrow.' The foreman gave his boss an admiring look. 'I'll hand it to you for some smart thinkin', Stormy. If we hadn't gone scoutin' up on the War Dance it's a cinch Red Yessap would have wiped us out. Wouldn't have been a man-jack of the outfit left to tell the tale.'

Storm refused to take any credit. It was the Winston girl's story that had aroused his suspicions against Ed Manners.

'Mebbe so'—Jim spoke dryly—'Mebbe she *did* give you the idee to scout 'round up on the War Dance, but it wasn't her that framed up this play to trap Manners an' Yessap with their own bait.'

They jogged up the dusty street and drew rein in front of Dave's barn. A Mexican watched them from under the spreading glow of a big lamp swung from a beam above the door. The boss had gone to supper, he informed them.

The tired horses were led into the barn and unsaddled. The Mexican climbed up to the loft and pitched hay down into the mangers. He'd give them grain later, when they'd cooled off, he told Storm. Had the señores heard about Johnny? *Por Dios!* It was bad business!

Storm and Jim agreed that it was bad business. The news about Johnny was going to hit the boys hard. Johnny was popular, always took good care of a man's horse.

'We'll be back in about an hour,' Storm told the Mexican. 'Got to get started for the ranch soon as we've had supper—and a talk with Dave.'

Jim Race crossed the street and vanished inside the saloon. Storm mounted the porch steps to the lobby of the Stagg House. He was dusty from the long day in the hills and spent a few minutes in the washroom. Mrs. Stagg greeted him from the dining-room door when he leisurely made his way back to the lobby.

'Saw you come in, Stormy. Knew you'd want to clean up a bit or I'd have called out for you to come right in to supper.'

'Hello, Sarah!' Storm gave Dave's buxom wife an affectionate smile. He was fond of Mrs. Stagg.

'Jim Race will be along in a few minutes. Dropped in at the bar for a drink.'

Mrs. Stagg showed some surprise. 'Jim don't usually hanker for whiskey,' she commented with a disapproving shake of her head.

'Well, Sarah, between you and me it was some business took Jim over there.'

'Don't you go to thinkin' I'm jumping on him for wantin' a drink.' Mrs. Stagg shook her head again. 'It's just that I've got no use for that saloon Ed Manners runs. Don't like Ed Manners an' never will. He's plain low-down.' Mrs. Stagg lowered her voice. 'Stormy—is it true—what Dave's been tellin' me about the Winston girl? Is she really stayin' out to the ranch?'

'We're not saying much about it, Sarah. Don't want to start talk.' Storm guessed that Dave had not told his wife the details. The old man was given to discreet silences.

'Poor child,' commiserated Mrs. Stagg. 'Must have been a shock, Baldy throwin' her like he did. Was she hurt, Stormy?'

'Ynes put her to bed,' Storm told her innocently.

'Poor child,' repeated Mrs. Stagg. She looked hard at him. 'I'll bet Ynes was awful surprised.'

'She was fine about it,' Storm said simply.

A romantic look crept into Mrs. Stagg's eyes. 'Ynes has always been after you to get some nice girl into that house. It's real excitin'—you findin' Miss Winston like you did an' takin' her to your home. Ynes'll say it's an answer to prayer.'

'You're silly.' Storm reddened.

Mrs. Stagg looked at him intently. 'She believes in miracles, Ynes does.' Storm's visible embarrassment checked her. She gave him an amused smile. 'You'll be wantin' your supper, Stormy.'

'Always hungry when I come to the Stagg House,' grinned Storm. 'Got apple pie, tonight? Jim Race says he has a "hankerin'" for apple pie—the kind you make.'

'Bless the man's heart!' Mrs. Stagg flushed with pleasure. 'I'm that glad I followed my hunch. Got a bakin' of the best apple pies I ever turned out of the oven.'

'Jim will founder himself,' predicted Storm. 'Jim's got no control when he comes to the Stagg House.'

'Burl Jenners come in on the stage,' Mrs. Stagg informed him. 'He's in the dinin'-room now, an' Pete Kendall with him, both of 'em settin' with Dave.'

'Plenty room for you to set with us, Stormy,' called Dave. 'Burl says he wants to talk with you.'

Storm pulled out the remaining chair. 'Wasn't expecting you back in town so soon, Burl.' He was wondering at the cattle-buyer's grim face. 'Looking awfully solemn,' he added. 'Some low-down cowman unload a bunch of scrubs on you?'

Jenners said curtly, 'You'd look solemn, too,

Stormy, if you knew what brings me back to Mesalta.'

'You mean our deal has fallen down?' Storm lost his smile. 'I'd hate that—right now.'

'Not that, Stormy.' Jenners lifted a protesting hand. 'You can bank on me—if you deliver the stuff.'

'You almost took my appetite away,' grumbled Storm. He smiled up at the approaching waitress. 'Make mine the same, Jenny, and be sure and save me a piece of apple pie.'

'Yes, Mr. MacKenzie.' Jenny dimpled, sped away with a rustle of crisply starched skirts.

Storm looked at Jenners. 'Well—what's this bad news?'

'Won't say it's *bad* news,' Jenners answered.

'I'd call it dynamite for Ed Manners if it's true,' put in Pete Kendall. 'Sure will blow him off the map if what Burl's got on the skunk holds water.'

Dave Stagg nodded agreement. 'Means Ed's finish in this town.'

'We can't be certain until Fred Morton gets here,' Jenners continued. 'Fred won't be in for a day or two, maybe tomorrow evenin's stage.'

'Who's Fred Morton?' Storm was getting impatient.

'Fred's a Pinkerton man I was talkin' to back in Kansas City.'

Storm stared. '*Pinkerton* man?' His tone was startled. 'What's up, Burl?'

'Plenty. If Fred's guessin' right, your leading cit-

174

izen, Mr. Ed Manners, is a forger known to the police as Ed Mertz. The Pinkertons have been on his trail for years.'

Dave Stagg's chuckle broke the silence. 'Stormy looks like a mule has landed both hind legs plumb center to the stummick.'

'I was thinking about something,' Storm said in a harsh voice. 'What Burl says about Ed Manners's being a forger begins to clear up a mystery that's been bothering me.'

'There's a chance Fred's wrong,' Jenners cautioned him. 'Nothin' we can do until Fred Morton gets here with the proof.'

'Vin Terrill will baulk plenty,' observed Dave. 'Vin won't want to arrest Ed.'

'Fred won't need the sheriff. It's federal business. Fred will make the arrest. Don't you worry.' Jenners's eyes gleamed as Jenny came up with a laden tray. 'Ah, the apple pie, and *what* a pie!'

Jenny giggled. 'Mrs. Stagg says there's plenty more.'

'I'm goin' to retire,' declared Mr. Jenners. 'I'm goin' to come an' live at the Stagg House.'

Jim Race clattered in from the lobby and took a chair at the adjoining table. 'You go easy on that pie, Burl,' he begged. 'Give me a chance to git my rope on a few pieces.'

'Hello, you old sidewinder!' Jenners glared at the foreman. 'You keep off my range. Won't stand for nobody rustlin' my pie.'

'Speakin' of snakes'—Jim lowered his voice—'just run into Ed Manners an' Vin Terrill over in the saloon.' The foreman sent a grin at Storm. 'Was tellin' Ed we'd be startin' the drive tomorrow. Ed was mighty interested. Said he was wonderin' what Burl was back in town so quick for.'

The cattle-buyer turned a surprised look on Storm. 'I don't want them steers yet, Stormy. I told you ninety days.'

'Don't get excited, Burl.' Storm's smile was grim. 'I've reasons for wanting Ed to think the drive starts tomorrow. Don't you tell anybody different. Might spoil certain plans.'

The other men stared at him curiously. Dave Stagg's one eye gleamed as though he divined what was in Storm's mind. He nodded approval. 'You've got a head on your shoulders, son,' he drawled. 'Don't quite savvy your play, but I'm thinkin' you're baitin' a trap to catch you a wolf.'

'A pack of 'em,' muttered Jim Race. 'Leave it to Stormy to think up tricks.'

'I don't know'—Storm spoke thoughtfully. 'I may be wrong, but I've a hunch I'm on the right track.' He looked at Burl Jenners. 'You may be wrong, too, but if you're right about Manners's being what Fred Morton claims, I've another hunch worth looking into.'

'What do you mean?' queried Jenners.

'I was thinking it would be easy for an expert forger to sign a man's name to a deed to his ranch and get away with it—if the man happened to be dead.'

There was a silence, broken by an angry growl from Dave Stagg.

'The snake,' he muttered, 'the crawlin' sidewinder. You got to stomp on his ugly head, Stormy.'

'I intend to,' Storm said. His face was suddenly hard.

18
A Life at Stake

SHERIFF TERRILL had the look of a man who was stalking a notoriously ferocious grizzly bear. He was not liking the job of placing Storm MacKenzie under arrest. The chances were good that Storm's reactions would be prompt and devastatingly violent.

The sheriff halted under the glow of the big swing lamp and peered apprehensively into the stable, dimly lighted by a lantern that hung on a peg. He knew that Storm was in one of the stalls, and for the moment was alone. The sheriff had been watching from behind a straw pile when Storm came from the Stagg House. The young rancher had paused for a word with the Mexican stableman loafing in Dave's chair in front of the entrance and then disappeared into the barn. A moment later the Mexican got out of the chair and crossed over to the little cantina opposite.

The set-up was ideal for the purpose in Terrill's mind. He had Storm cornered, and alone. If he worked fast nobody would know what had happened.

Storm was suddenly coming toward him, leading his brown horse. His face lifted in a surprised look at the sheriff.

'Hello, Terrill!'

The sheriff disregarded the unfriendly tone. 'Lucky I seen you comin' over from the Stagg House. Was about to look in there for you.'

Storm's eyebrows raised inquiringly. 'What's on your mind?'

'Got a feller in jail would like you to take a look at. Picked him up an hour or two back.'

'What's it got to do with me?' Storm wanted to know. It was in his mind that the sheriff was slightly drunk.

'Plenty,' hiccoughed the sheriff. 'Stan James claims he's one of the fellers that was with Red Yessap the day Red pulled his gun on you here in the street.' Terrill stole a sideways look at the cantina across the street. No sign of the Mexican yet. 'Thought mebbe you'd know this feller if you took a look at him.'

'I'd know him,' admitted Storm. He hesitated, glanced up the street.

'Won't take but a few minutes,' the sheriff pointed out.

'I'm waiting for Jim,' Storm informed him.

'We're riding back to the ranch, just as soon as he gets over from the hotel.'

'Won't take but a few minutes to look at this jasper,' repeated the sheriff. 'You'll be back at the barn by the time Jim gits here, most likely.' Terrill teetered on his heels, frowned importantly. 'It's your dooty to aid the law, Stormy. If you back up what Stan says I'm sendin' this jasper over to the county jail to stand trial.'

Storm knew Stan James, the local town marshal. Stan was a fairly efficient officer and owed his appointment to Storm and a few others of the more prominent cattlemen who were anxious for their riders to have fair play when they came to spend their money in Mesalta.

'Stan's over at the jail now,' Terrill urged. 'All I want is for you to back him up an' I'll hold this feller for trial.'

'All right,' finally agreed Storm. 'Wonder where that Mexican went to. He could tell Jim.'

'Seen the Mex headin' up the street some place.' Terrill spoke impatiently. He was getting nervous. 'Come on, Stormy. No sense wastin' time leavin' word for Jim. You'll be back in no time.'

Without further protest Storm accompanied the sheriff past the wide front of the barn and up the dark narrow street toward the jail that stood in a small clearing between the town and the river. The brown horse followed on a lead-rope.

The easy climb seemed to trouble the sheriff, made

him puff and blow. Storm looked at him once or twice. Terrill was more drunk than he had thought.

'Gittin' so I lose my wind awful quick,' bemoaned the sheriff, secretly worried by Storm's several glances. So far he had managed the affair smoothly. 'Mighty fine of you to help me on this thing, Stormy.'

The jail stood in darkness, save for the pale glow of a lamp in the office window. Terrill pushed the door open, motioned for Storm to enter. 'Stan's waitin' in the office,' he said.

Storm walked in, came to an abrupt standstill. Stan James was not in the office, but backed up against the wall, leveled rifles in their hands, were three men. Something hard pressed against his spine, he heard Terrill's voice, drunkenly triumphant.

'I'll blow you to pieces, Stormy, if you make a move.'

Storm found his voice. 'What are you trying to do, Terrill?'

The sheriff's gun pressed harder. 'Git his Colt, Frenchy.'

Frenchy obeyed, snatched the weapon from holster and placed it on the table. Terrill spoke again. 'Git movin', Stormy. I'm lockin' you up.'

Resistance was suicide. Storm walked on through the office and up the corridor. A man waited there by an open cell door. His face seemed vaguely familiar. He motioned to the cell. Storm walked inside, heard the door clang shut.

Terrill and his four aides were shapeless blurs in the dim light of the lantern in the hand of the man who had motioned him into the cell. The sheriff was speaking, his face pressed close to the bars. 'Only way to git you without bloodshed, Stormy.'

Storm stared at them, cold contempt in his eyes. Frenchy Jack, he knew. Two of the others were strangers. He bent his look on the man with the lantern. He knew now why the latter's face was familiar. He had seen him before, the night of the attempt to ambush him on the Juniper Flats trail. Vordal's brutish-faced companion. Storm's blood chilled. Something was decidedly wrong. This was no lawful occasion. Terrill had tricked him nicely.

'Pulled a good one on you, huh, Stormy?' The renegade sheriff grinned round at his companions. 'Saved us plenty gunplay. Figgered Stormy wouldn't take arrest easy an' sensible.'

'Arrest?' Storm's voice was harsh with anger. 'Am I to understand this is an arrest?'

Terrill laughed drunkenly. 'You're behind the bars, ain't you?' He grew belligerent. 'Sure it's an arrest. I'm arrestin' you for kidnappin' Miss Winston. Her ma has sworn to the charge.'

'Somebody's crazy,' muttered Storm.

'No chance for you to git out of this jail,' Terrill went on. 'Your friends won't think of lookin' for you here. When I git back from the ranch with the gal I'll take you over to the county jail and hold you for trial.'

'You mean that, Terrill?' Storm managed to keep his voice quiet. He wanted to shout curses at the drunken fool. 'You—you're going to bring Miss Winston back to this town?'

'Sure I am. Was only waitin' to git you landed in jail.' The sheriff pushed his gun back into holster, teetered on his heels. 'You're in a tight fix, Stormy. Folks in this county won't like this kidnappin' bus'ness. You'll be lucky if they don't come an' break you out of this jail an' string you up. Kidnappin' is nigh as bad as cow-stealin'.'

'You're drunk, and a fool to boot,' Storm told him furiously.

Terrill glared at him. 'Huh, insultin' the sheriff, usin' vile an' obscene talk to a officer of the law that's engaged in doin' his sworn dooty. I'll have a fine slapped on ag'in you for that, mister.'

'Ed Manners put you up to this.'

'Ed ain't got a thing to do with me throwin' you in jail!' shouted Terrill. 'You're barkin' up the wrong tree.'

'I'll tell you now that Miss Winston won't leave the ranch, come back with you to this town.' Storm was fighting a growing panic. 'I didn't kidnap the girl.'

'Ain't expectin' you to admit you did.' The sheriff laughed unpleasantly.

'Let me talk to Mrs. Winston,' Storm said desperately.

'She wouldn't believe you on a stack o' Bibles,'

sneered Terrill. 'She's the one that's charged you with the crime.'

'Get Lester Warde over here,' urged Storm.

'Huh! Warde would likely kill you. Miss Winston's his gal. Warde's fit to be tied.'

'You can't keep me in this jail,' argued Storm. 'I've a right to bail.'

'It'll be up to the judge when I git you over to the county seat.' Terrill was losing his patience. 'Ain't wastin' no more time with you, Stormy. I'm off for the ranch with my deputies.'

'Miss Winston won't leave the ranch. You can't make her.'

'What she wants makes no difference,' retorted the sheriff. 'She's comin' no matter what she says. Her ma's signed a warrant.'

Storm found himself wordless. As from afar he heard the sheriff's drink-thickened voice.

'I'm leavin' Ducker keep guard on you,' Terrill was saying. 'You won't be seein' Stan James. Stan's went to Phoenix, which is why I got the run of his jail. Ain't no prisoner here but you, Stormy.' Terrill chuckled. 'You won't be lonesome; Ducker'll stick close.'

The man holding the lantern grinned. 'Closer'n a tick sticks to a dog's hind laig,' he assured the sheriff. 'Git goin' when you want, Vin. I'll keep this polecat safe for you.'

Storm listened impotently to the clatter of booted feet down the corridor. The door closed with a bang.

The thought of Fanny Winston's peril sent a wave of horror through Storm. The kidnapping charge was trumped up to get him out of the way, a scheme to throw the girl into Manners's hands. Mrs. Winston may have acted innocently enough, but she would never see her daughter alive again. Those men Terrill was using as deputies would have their orders. Fanny's fate would be sealed if she left the ranch in the company of Frenchy Jack and his murderous companions.

The minutes dragged by—wretched, torturing minutes—and suddenly the corridor door opened, let in a faint light. Ducker, coming, lantern in hand. Storm was conscious of cold prickles as he watched the approaching man. Ducker—one of the men who had followed him on the Juniper Flats trail. A hireling killer.

Storm began to see more deeply into the plot. Ducker was to keep him safe in the jail. Ducker's story would be simple. The prisoner shot while attempting to break jail. The man would be within the law in obeying the orders of the county sheriff. Not even the sheriff would know that murder had been done, a murder cunningly contrived by Ed Manners. Storm was certain of Ducker's purpose.

The man was peering at him, lantern held high in hand. He spoke curtly, words so astonishing that Storm could only stare, himself speechless.

'I'm turnin' you loose, MacKenzie. Hell's like to break any moment. Wasn't bargainin' to fight off a mob,' he added.

'A mob?' Storm looked at the man incredulously.

'Looks like it's leaked out we've got you here in jail. Makes it tough.'

'You mean a mob is coming to get me?'

Ducker swore at him. 'That's what I said. They're fixin' up a necktie party.'

'Get me out of here,' Storm begged. He watched the deputy closely, aware of a curious tenseness in the man.

'Sure,' grunted Ducker. 'Let's git this bus'ness done with.' His key turned in the lock. He stepped back, gun in hand, motioned with the lantern for Storm to precede him down the corridor.

Storm hesitated. The distance was too great for a flying tackle, a lightning grab for the gun.

'Where's my horse?' He was in the corridor now, face turned toward the watchful-eyed deputy.

'Ain't sure. Reckon Terrill took him over to Ed's barn.' Ducker's lips twisted in a mirthless smile. 'No chance for you to git your horse. Best thing you can do is make a quick sneak into the brush. Ed always keeps a night man at the barn. He'd nab you sure.'

Storm moved down the corridor. The thought of the gun behind him unpleasantly chilled his spine. He knew Ducker was lying about a mob coming to lynch him. The man was carefully following instructions. The murder was to present all the details of an attempted escape.

The office door stood open, a lighted lamp on the table. Storm's feet moved more slowly. Intuition warned him it was in the office that the crucial moment would come.

A gun lay on the table. His own Colt, still lying where Frenchy Jack had placed it. One more stride and the weapon would be in his hand. Something stopped him, stayed the impulse to reach for the gun. It was too convenient.

His lagging feet came to a standstill within a scant two feet from the table. He knew Ducker was framed in the corridor door behind him, heard the faint clank of the lantern on the floor. Storm had no need to look. The mirror on the opposite wall showed Ducker stepping closer, gun lifting in his hand, squat face suddenly set in a taut grimace of triumph. He was waiting for the expected reaching of hand for the gun on the table.

Storm stood there. He had seen dangerous moments before. None quite so hair-raising as this, nor had his mind ever worked so coolly, his nerves been so steady. He heard his voice, quiet, cheerful, ringing with gratitude. 'You're a good scout, Ducker. Worth a thousand dollars to me—this chance to get away.'

An impatient grunt came from Ducker. He wanted Storm to reach for that gun. His prisoner's easy assurance, his talk about a thousand dollars' worth of gratitude, distracted his attention from his grim purpose. Storm, watching in the mirror, saw the man's momentary hesitation. His hand, not the one nearest the gun on the table, swept out in a swinging motion that lifted the glass lamp and hurled it full in Ducker's face.

There was no time for the horrified deputy to dodge. The lamp, flaring madly, caught him squarely on the side of the head and burst into flames. The gun dropped from his hand. He screamed, began to beat at the flames that seized hold of his kerosene-soaked clothes. The next instant the fallen gun was in Storm's hands. He pushed the weapon into his holster and gave his attention to what promised to be a human torch.

Ducker was out of his senses with fear and agony. He ran wildly up the corridor, moaning and sobbing and tearing frantically at his burning shirt.

A slicker hung from a peg on the office wall. Storm snatched it, went swiftly in pursuit. It was too horrible to let the man suffer. And his mad flight was making matters worse, fanning the red tongues of fire. He was suddenly down on the floor, clawing at his tortured face, writhing and twisting and moaning.

Storm flung the slicker over him, rolled him in it. He was conscious of burnt hair and flesh, the stench of burning wool. He was sickened, but felt no remorse. The man would have murdered him.

He had done the one thing possible to save his own life—to save Fanny Winston.

He jerked the whimpering Ducker to his feet, held him with one hand against the wall, free hand resting on the butt of the holstered gun.

'I should kill you,' he said.

Fright and pain had taken all the fight out of the man. One of his eyes was a swollen blister, the hair on the same side of his head burned to a crisp, and a great red streak down his cheek showed the course of the flaming kerosene.

Storm studied him closely in the dim light from the lantern standing on the floor lower down the corridor. Ducker was in bad shape, but still capable of causing trouble once he was over his fright. Time was too precious to waste giving him first aid. Nor dare he turn the man loose. Ducker would lose no time in giving the alarm.

The cell door still hung open, the key in the lock outside. Storm pulled Ducker away from the wall, pushed him into the cell and slammed the door.

'You ain't leavin' me here,' whined the deputy. 'Gawd—I need a doc . . . my eye's burnt out—' He broke off in a whimper.

Storm turned the key. 'Nothing else I can do, Ducker,' he said harshly. 'Your own fault.' He ran down the corridor, pausing to pick up the lantern, which he placed on the table. His look went to the Colt lying there. He took the gun in his hands. No cartridges in the chambers, and the gun had been fully loaded when Frenchy Jack took it from him. Storm thanked his lucky star that had kept him from seizing the gun so temptingly placed for his hand. The picture was plain. He would have faced Ducker with an empty gun, taken the man's bullets without a chance to fire a shot. Ed Manners must have framed the plot. Ducker hadn't the brains. The story would have gone out that Storm MacKenzie had been killed while making a desperate attempt to break jail.

He reloaded the Colt from the cartridges in his belt, blew out the lantern, and hurried into the darkness of the night.

The thought of the brown horse, virtually a prisoner in Ed Manners's stable, worried Storm. He could get a horse from Dave Stagg's livery barn, but he wanted Cacique for the fast hard ride to the ranch. He knew Cacique's qualities. The brown horse had speed and stamina possessed by no animal in Dave's barn. Also Storm had a fondness for Cacique that made him reluctant to leave him in the hands of his enemy. Ed Manners would lose no time in smuggling the horse out of the country.

Storm came to a standstill at the foot of the hill. He could see the lamp still burning in front of the Palace Bar. Dave's livery barn was in darkness. Dave must have been puzzled by his sudden disappearance. Jim Race, too. He suspected that Terrill probably would have told Dave's Mexican that he'd seen Storm heading for the ranch. The

Mexican knew Storm had gone into the barn to throw his saddle on Cacique. Terrill's story that he had left for the ranch without waiting for Jim would seem credible. Jim Race would be puzzled, but not too surprised. The foreman was not one to question anything his boss chose to do. Also Jim was not intending to accompany him all the way to the home ranch. They would have parted when they reached Los Gatos Canyon, where Jim took the lower trail to the cattle camp.

The moon was tipping the hills. Storm judged he must have been almost an hour in the jail. Terrill and his dubious deputies would be nearing the ranch. They would be sure to take the long road.

In less than half a minute he was moving quickly across the dark street and into a gully that he knew twisted around back of the Palace Hotel. Ed Manners's barn stood in a clearing some hundred yards from the hotel and close to the gully. Thanks to Ducker he knew a night man was on duty.

Five minutes brought him within sight of the stable. He watched for a few moments. The place was in darkness. No sign of a light. Storm began to wonder if Ducker had lied about the night man. He drew his gun, went swiftly to the door and pulled. A chain held it fast on the inside.

Something stirred beyond the door, a man's voice called out peevishly.

'Open up.' Storm did his best to imitate Ed Manners's voice. It was not a very good imitation, but the hostler was obviously too sleepy to notice, and a horse stamping restlessly in one of the stalls made it difficult for him to hear plainly.

'Just a moment, boss—' Storm heard the shuffling of feet over straw, the chain rattled down from the hook and the door swung out, revealed the face of a shock-headed man peering through the opening. 'Wasn't expectin' a call from you tonight, boss—' The man broke off with a startled grunt, a look of horror freezing his unshaven face. Something hard was pressing against his stomach.

No word was needed from Storm. The aghast hostler lifted his hands high. The smell of instant death was in his nostrils and he didn't like it.

The door swung wide open, caught on the catch-peg set in the ground. Pale moonlight flowed in.

'Turn 'round,' Storm ordered curtly. 'No more talk.'

The man obeyed. The look in Storm's eyes was like a blow.

A coil of rope hung on a peg. Storm snatched it down, pushed the hostler roughly into a vacant stall.

He made a thorough job of tying the man and left him lying on the straw, his own bandanna bound securely over his mouth. Scarcely three minutes had elapsed since the door had swung open. The fretful horse was still stamping restlessly. The sound drew Storm like a magnet. Cacique wasn't liking his strange quarters, and he knew that his master was close.

Saddle and bridle hung from a peg behind the stall. Storm threw on the saddle, drew the cinch lightly, and carrying the bridle he hurriedly led the horse into the moonlit night. Despite his anxiety to get away from the place he stopped to push the door shut and snap the outside catch. In another minute a growth of scrubby piñons hid him and the horse from chance eyes.

The big brown gelding nickered softly, rubbed Storm's arm with velvety muzzle. Storm drew on the bridle, tightened the cinch, and flung himself into the saddle.

Less than twenty minutes had passed since leaving Ducker locked up in the cell. The man must be suffering. But the life of Fanny Winston was in the balance. He could not afford to waste pity on Ducker.

He kept the brown horse moving at a fast running-walk, following the twisting course of the gully until the few lights in the town winked out behind the ridge. He would have liked a word with Dave Stagg. The risk was too great. He had a job to do. Every minute counted. Terrill would be taking the long road. He would not hurry. Storm MacKenzie was in jail, unable to stay the sheriff from his mission.

Cacique went up the trail without a falter in his smooth distance-eating running-walk. Suddenly they were on the flats, the trail reaching straight as an arrow toward the Los Gatos ridge. Storm's spurs raked the satiny sides. No mercy for horse or himself this night.

19
The Sheriff Pays a Call

FUGITIVE gleams of sunlight still lingered in the garden, danced through the leaves of the poplars, made an ever-shifting filigree of gold across the path. A soft breeze whispered through the tall pines under which the girl stood.

Fanny liked the old garden. There was peace here—a feeling of security. She felt she never wanted to see Mesalta again, at least not while men like Ed Manners lived there.

Just what to do was a problem. Her mother would think she was quite mad, would never believe her story of the weird plot against her life. Nor would Lester Warde.

Storm MacKenzie was more than kind. He would not listen to her proposal that she go back to town.

Her thoughts went to the slain Johnny. When the time came she was resolved to tell all she knew. Manners was the *real* murderer, Vordal only an instrument in his hand. Her story could hang Manners. She was a menace the man would not endure.

Her face lifted in a look at the tall pines. They stood like sentinels on either side of a small gate set in a hedge that enclosed what was obviously a tiny graveyard.

The hedge was higher than her head and covered with masses of yellow roses. She picked one, fastened it in the low-cut bodice of her dress. It was a quaint, old-fashioned dress of soft green muslin with full beruffled skirt, one of the dresses Ynes had given her to replace the torn, rain-soaked riding habit. Ynes had been all kindness, in fact seemed to take an enormous satisfaction in making her comfortable.

She moved to the gate of the little enclosure. Flowers, a plot of grass, some shrubs—two graves side by side. Fanny divined it was here that Storm MacKenzie's parents rested.

Footsteps approaching down the path from the house swung her around. Ynes, a basket on her arm, a pair of scissors in her hand.

The Mexican woman came to a standstill a few feet away, looked at her intently. Fanny smiled at her nervously, wondered if she was annoyed to find her looking into the graveyard.

Ynes spoke softly. 'Eet geeve me queer feel, señorita, for see you stan' there. You make me theenk of the señora who now lie in the leetle garden.'

'Mr. MacKenzie's mother?' The girl's look went to the graves.

'*Si*'—Ynes nodded. 'Stormito's mother, an' close by her side as he was always in life, lie the old señor. God rest their souls.' She crossed herself devoutly. '*Si*—I 'ave the queer feel to see you stan' there in her dress. The old señor like that dress so mooch.'

'It's a lovely dress,' agreed Fanny. She looked down at the beruffled skirt. 'We must have been about the same size. It fits me perfectly.'

'*Si*, you 'ave same size,' confirmed Ynes. 'She 'ave nize shape—like you.'

Fanny was amused. 'You'll make me vain.'

Ynes's placid smile showed she was not alarmed. 'You 'ave 'air same as señora's,' she went on, 'nize 'air—like wing of blackbird in sunlight.'

'It's just plain black.'

'Stormito will stare w'en he see you in that dress,' Ynes said musingly.

Fanny felt suddenly conscious. 'Perhaps he won't—won't like me wearing his—his mother's dress.'

'I would not let *any* girl wear that dress.' Ynes's voice took on a curiously hushed note. '*Si*—the miracle 'ave come—the miracle I pray for to the Blessed Virgin.'

'The miracle?' Fanny's tone was puzzled. 'I don't understand, Ynes.'

The old housekeeper smiled indulgently. 'You 'ave no need onderstan', señorita.' She began clipping the yellow roses.

195

'Let me hold the basket,' begged the girl.

The roses, so early and so many, also indicated a favorable portent, Ynes told Fanny. Stormito's mother had brought the first cuttings with her from Texas when she was a bride. The roses had not done so well since her death, but within the week the hedge had become a mass of blooms. The same with the parent vine on the north wall of the *casa*. A wonderful omen that her many prayers were answered. '*Si*'—in response to the girl's question.—The señora had died when Stormito was still a youth. Stormito and the old señor had made the little garden and planted the hedge of yellow roses—cuttings from the vines she had loved and tended so carefully.

They went slowly back to the house, through the deepening twilight, the filled basket in the girl's hand. She was mystified by the old woman's talk of omens and the miracle that was to make great changes in the life of the old *rancho*. Fanny's first inclination to smile gradually gave way to fascinated attention. Ynes was too much in earnest to be merely amusing.

The evening was balmy, pleasant enough to sit out on the veranda. Tomasa brought a small table and spread a snowy cloth. Ynes appeared in the doorway.

'Stormito like eat outside w'en eet ees warm,' she told Fanny. 'You like—no?'

Fanny expressed her pleasure, and presently

Tomasa appeared with a tray on which was a plate of fried chicken with rice and cream gravy. Ynes followed with biscuits hot from the oven and a pot of coffee.

The girl ate slowly. She was wishing she could talk to Storm MacKenzie. She had scarcely seen him since the day he had brought her to the ranch. She guessed that her story about Ed Manners and Red Yessap was worrying him. Ynes wasn't sure, but she thought he and Jim Race were looking things over in Red Canyon Corral. They had ridden with the dawn. Storm had left word he would have supper in town and wouldn't be home until late. Jim Race would be returning to the cattle camp somewhere on the Little Mesalta.

Fanny guessed Storm and the foreman planned to do some investigating in Red Canyon. She felt nervous about it. There was a chance they would run into Red Yessap.

From the bunkhouse, hidden by the trees, came intermittent snatches of song to the accompaniment of a guitar. The two cowboys with the queer names. Jericho, and Sooner Bass. One or the other of them was never far away. Fanny had a suspicion they were obeying orders. Storm feared for her safety, but didn't want her to know she was being guarded.

Fanny no longer attempted to keep her thoughts away from Storm. She was thinking of him constantly, found pleasure in letting her mind dwell on all the scraps of information Ynes dropped about him. She wondered if Ynes was noticing her little probings, her skillfully artless questions about Storm.

A duet was now in full swing over at the bunkhouse, something about a lone cowboy who lay dying somewhere west of Pecos. It was a very sad song, and Jericho's tenor worked up heartrendingly. Cowboys seemed to like sad songs.

Jericho was Fanny's favorite. She enjoyed his happy-go-lucky cheeriness. Nothing bashful about the red-headed young cowboy. He was friendly, without being familiar, easy to talk to and full of interesting tales of the cattle range. Sooner Bass was less obvious, taciturn and grim of face. Fanny was the least bit afraid of him. He had a curiously disconcerting unwinking stare and habitually wore two guns in his holsters. She wondered at the close companionship of this hard, ruthless-appearing person and the laughing-eyed Jericho. No doubt but what Sooner's looks and manner were against him. He must be all right, or Storm MacKenzie wouldn't have him around.

She had puzzled a bit over their names. The reason for the 'Sooner' was easy to understand after a few minutes' talk with him. Sooner Bass would sooner do anything than do it.

Jericho was a mystery still unsolved. Fanny reminded herself to ask Storm MacKenzie. She couldn't believe that Jericho was actually the red-headed cowboy's name.

Tomasa appeared, removed the tray and table. Fanny changed to the big manzanita chair. The moon was lifting over the mountains, threw a lacework of shadows across the patio garden. The pale glow caught one of the big pine timbers that supported the veranda roof, drew the girl's eyes to the curious mark burned deep into the rich yellow patina. She puzzled over it for a few moments. Suddenly she got the meaning, the mark of the Diamond M—the MacKenzie cattle brand.

Fanny found herself wondering about the diamond part of the brand. She could understand why the M was used. M stood for MacKenzie. She was vaguely aware that a cattleman's iron mark had some significant meaning. No doubt there was a good reason for the MacKenzie Diamond M.

Ynes made her noiseless appearance, stood smiling at her. '*Si*—eet ees Stormito's mark. The old señor put the 'ot iron into hees han' . . . told heem to burn deep.' Her tone was reminiscent.

'I can't make out what the diamond means,' puzzled the girl.

'The señora geeve the señor her diamonds for buy the cow w'en they come from Texas. She hees yong wife . . . she ver' mooch love the señor. He make Diamond M brand because he mooch 'appy to buy the cow for *rancho*.' Ynes nodded emphatically. '*Muy bueno!*'

'It's a sweet story.' Fanny spoke softly. 'She must have loved him—trusted him. I'm glad you told me,' she added. 'It makes it seem more than just a cattle brand. Mr. MacKenzie must be proud of his Diamond M.'

'Stormito love the *rancho*.' Ynes looked at the girl intently. 'I tell heem to get wife queek now. Stormito mus' 'ave son to burn mark on post.' Ynes shook her head sadly. 'Stormito ver' slow. . . . I make mooch prayer for miracle.' She crossed herself, added in a brightening tone, 'The miracle 'ave come.'

Fanny gave her a startled look. She was beginning to understand. Ynes saw her confusion, showed some alarm. She must not force the unfolding of the miracle for which she had prayed so faithfully. 'We leave these things to the Good God,' she said gently in Spanish.

The words were meaningless to the girl, but something she saw in the old Mexican woman's eyes, the simplicity of the utterance, gave her a vague understanding. She relaxed in the big chair, smiled faintly. 'You are very sweet, Ynes. We're going to be good friends.'

'*Si*'—Ynes's face was radiant—'*muy simpatica.*'

'Yes'—Fanny only vaguely grasped her meaning. 'We feel the same way about—about lots of things.'

'*Si—muy simpatica*—we theenk ver' cloze—we beeg frien'.'

'I like you,' declared Fanny.

'*Gracias.*' Ynes smiled, a fond look in her fine

dark eyes. 'W'en I see you come weeth Stormito I know miracle 'ave 'appen'.'

'You are very romantic,' laughed the girl. She was glad her face was in the shadow of the big post.

'No!' Ynes shook her head, turned to the door. 'My 'eart no lie.' She vanished into the hall.

Fanny lay back in the chair, lifted burning cheeks to the cool breeze. She wasn't sure whether to be indignant or amused. The thing was too absurd. Sweet of Ynes, though, to have such thoughts about her. Her hand toyed with the ruffles of the soft green skirt. Stormito's mother had worn it. *I would not let any girl wear that dress.* But Ynes had wanted Fanny to wear it. Fanny was the longed-for miracle—the girl Ynes wanted for her Stormito's wife.

Fanny came to with a start. Somebody was driving into the ranch yard. She could hear the rattle of buckboard wheels, the thud of hoofs as the team swung through the gate. The girl lifted her head. It wouldn't be Storm MacKenzie so early. Anyway he wouldn't be driving home in a buggy. Fanny's heart stood still. Not unless something had happened and he was being *brought* home.

Voices reached her, a man's gruff, barking tones, an answer from somebody at the bunkhouse door. Jericho's voice. Fanny got out of the chair, stood listening.

'What you want with her, sheriff?' The laughter was gone from Jericho's voice.

'Her ma sent me.'

'Reckon you'll have to wait till the boss gets back,' Jericho replied.

Fanny came out of her chair. *The sheriff—with a message from her mother.* The girl considered swiftly. Storm had warned her to keep out of sight if strangers came around. But surely the sheriff would be a safe man. He represented the law—and she was not in hiding from the law.

Jericho was speaking again. 'Miss Winston ain't seein' nobody right now.'

Fanny came to a quick decision. 'I'll see the sheriff, Jericho,' she called out. 'Ask him to come in here.'

The sheriff's voice came back brusquely. 'I'll be right over, ma'am.'

Fanny heard the crunch of booted feet crossing the yard. She heard another sound. A shape hurried up the path from the small side gate near the bunkhouse. Sooner Bass, both guns in his holster. His dark face wore a troubled look as he mounted the veranda steps and crouched in the shadow of the climbing rosebush.

Fanny's eyes widened. 'Why—Sooner—' she began.

He shook his head. 'I'm stickin' here close.' He spoke in a harsh whisper. 'Ain't carin' for them fellers Terrill has with him.'

Fanny's look went apprehensively to the main yard gate. Several men were pushing through and approaching up the patio walk. Four of them! A lot of men just to bring a message from her mother.

Jericho suddenly appeared from the small gate, hurriedly ran up the steps and stood near her. Fanny was startled by the change in him. His face was a cold mask, his eyes hard, watchful.

Misgivings seized the girl. There was something terrifying about those approaching men. They were armed, decidedly frightening.

Terrill halted at the foot of the steps, looked up at her solemnly. 'Howdy, ma'am. Reckon you're Miss Fanny Winston, huh?'

Fanny inclined her head. She resented the man's gruff tone.

'Your ma sent me to git you,' the sheriff informed her. He scowled at Jericho. 'You keep out of this, young feller.'

'You've come to get me?' Fanny stared at him, shook her head. 'I'm sorry you've had all this trouble for nothing.'

'Huh?' The sheriff glowered. 'What you mean, ma'am?'

'I was under the impression you have a message for me from my mother.' Fanny spoke with quiet dignity. 'I don't like your talk about coming here to get me.'

'Sure I'm here to git you.' Terrill's tone was sour. 'Your ma's havin' fits about this bus'ness . . . wants you to come back to the hotel.'

'I'm sorry she's upset. I wish I *could* go to her.'

'I've got MacKenzie in jail,' Terrill told her. 'Won't stand for kidnappin' in *my* county.'

She gave him a shocked look. 'Kidnapping? What *are* you talking about?' The full import of the man's words was hitting her hard now. Storm MacKenzie was in jail . . . this sheriff was telling her that Storm was in jail—arrested for kidnapping her. 'You're crazy,' she stammered. 'You—you must all be mad. I wasn't kidnapped.'

Terrill looked at his companions, tapped his head significantly. 'Her ma said she mebbe would act queer. Must have been some shock—this kidnappin'.'

Jericho, standing close to the girl, said softly: 'We ain't lettin' him take you. Somethin' doggone smelly 'bout this bus'ness.'

She sent a brief glance in Sooner's direction. The cowboy was crouching behind the rosebush, as yet unseen by the sheriff and his men. Sooner's guns were no longer in the holsters. They were in his hands, ready for action.

The sheriff was speaking again, his voice harsh, impatient. 'Git your things, ma'am. Ain't wastin' no more time with you.' He moved nearer the steps. 'I'll go along with you in case you try some trick.'

'Keep away,' Fanny said fiercely. 'I'm not going with you! And you're lying about Mr. MacKenzie's being in jail.'

'He's in jail right enough.' Terrill's smile was

vicious. 'Ain't wastin' no more time,' he repeated.

'I'm not going with you,' reiterated the girl. 'I'm sure something is wrong. What's the idea of bringing an army with you? Am I some dangerous criminal?'

'These men are my deputies,' explained Terrill. 'Your ma said you might be touched in the head, so I brung 'em to help me if you got rough.'

There was a snort from Jericho. 'Some deputies,' muttered the cowboy. 'Some sheriff!'

Terrill fixed a stern eye on him. 'I've a notion to throw you in jail, too,' he threatened.

'You wont' throw nobody in jail, an' you ain't takin' Miss Winston from here, you ol' pot-bellied souse.'

The sheriff's face purpled with rage. 'Git that loudtalkin' jasper, fellers.' His hand reached to the gun in his holster. 'I'll 'tend to the girl.'

The forward surge of Frenchy Jack and his fellow-deputies halted at the foot of the steps. A low voice was addressing them.

'Cain't miss you from here, Terrill. I'm pullin' trigger—'

The sheriff's appalled look went to the vague shape behind the rosebush. His hand slid from gun-butt. 'Go easy, fellers. Looks like he's got the jump on us.'

There was a silence, broken by Sooner's chill voice. 'Git movin', Terrill, you an' your bunch o' jailbird deputies. French Jack's one of 'em, huh.

Last time I heard of Frenchy he was waitin' in a jail cell to be hung. Looks like Frenchy's broke jail.'

'You're makin' plenty trouble for yourself, Sooner,' warned Terrill. His fat red face was beaded with sweat. He knew Sooner's reputation with a gun. 'You'll land in jail, 'longside your boss, playin' the fool with your sheriff.'

'Git movin',' repeated Sooner Bass. 'Sure hate to mess up the boss's porch steps with a heap o' buzzard's meat.'

Jericho said softly to the girl, 'I'd go inside the house if I was you, Miss Winston. Sooner an' me will take care o' things.' He stood by her side, gun in hand, grinned cheerfully at the baffled posse. 'On your way, *Mister* Terrill. So glad you called, but right now our *Mister* Sooner Bass has got a awful itch in his trigger-finger. Got a notion I'm catchin' Sooner's itch.'

A shriek from the doorway drew all eyes. Ynes went charging down the steps, long full skirts billowing up like the feathers of an indignant hen defending her chicks. She pushed at the astonished sheriff, beat at him with her fists.

It was an unfortunate interruption. French Jack saw his chance. In a moment his hand was grasping her arm, his gun pressing into her side.

Jericho and Sooner could only stare in dismay. They knew Ynes would be the first to die if they attempted to shoot. The old housekeeper, suddenly aware of her blunder, began to sob. *'Ay, Dios mio!'* She sank on her knees, trembling lips moving in prayer.

'Drop your guns, boys.' There was relief in the sheriff's voice. 'We've got you licked.'

Fanny came out of her horrified daze. She looked at the two cowboys. 'Do as the man says,' she begged them. 'I won't have Ynes harmed.' Her voice broke. 'I—I'd rather go with them.'

'Reckon we're licked all right,' muttered Sooner Bass. He lowered his guns.

Jericho could only shake his head mournfully. Fear was in the look he sent at the girl. She knew it was fear for her.

'Get their guns,' Terrill said curtly.

One of the men gathered in the weapons. Terrill looked grimly at the two crestfallen Diamond M men. 'I'll go easy on you, boys. Ain't wantin' the bother of haulin' you back to town, so I'm lettin' you go free this time.'

Fanny interrupted fiercely. 'Tell that man to take his hands from Ynes.'

'Sure.' The sheriff spoke curtly to French Jack. The latter released his hold, swung his gun in the direction of Sooner Bass. 'For a red cent I'd empty it into your guts,' he said wrathfully.

'Please,' begged Fanny. She looked at the sheriff. 'I'll go with you . . . only I—I'd like to change my clothes.'

Terrill was in haste to get away while the cards

were in his hand. Sooner and Jericho were harmless for the moment, but the sheriff had heard things about the pair. They had an uncanny way of turning the tables, of doing the unexpected. The sheriff felt he was not going to rest easy until he had put a lot of distance between himself and the ranch. He shook his head. 'No more time to waste,' he said gruffly. 'You're comin' like you are.' His hand closed over her wrist.

The feel of his fingers made her go deathly pale. She wanted to scream. The look in his eyes was a ghastly revelation. The thing was a dreadful plot. Ed Manners was back of it—scheming to get his hands on her.

Fanny's look went to the door despairingly. She had felt so safe here in the old ranch-house, so secure from harm. It seemed she was wrong.

The sheriff was pulling her down the steps. He came to a sudden standstill, appeared to be listening. The other men listened, drawn guns in their hands. Fanny heard the sound now, the rhythmic beat made by the shod hoofs of a galloping horse.

'Somebody sure comin' like a bat out of hell.' Terrill's tone was uneasy.

'Headin' in across the pasture,' muttered French Jack. His gaze roved nervously toward the open patio gate. 'Let's git away from here, Vin.'

Fanny could see the pasture fence on the far side of the big yard. A rider was approaching. She couldn't be sure in the tricky moonlight, but yes—

yes—the rider was Storm MacKenzie. And he wasn't stopping to open any gates. The horse came over the fence without a falter.

Fanny heard her voice above the sudden uproar. *'Storm!'* she screamed, *'Storm—look out—they'll shoot!'*

20
One Against Four

THE sheriff's buckboard was standing at the hitch-rail under the big cottonwood tree. Vehicle and team stood out sharply against the moonlight that made a silver sea of the yard. The sight brought grim relief to Storm as he raced across the pasture. He was not too late.

Dust lifted, was snatched up by a flurry of wind in a whirling cloud. Somebody was screaming. Fanny Winston's voice, warning him to look out for trouble. Storm caught the flare of gunfire beyond the patio wall, heard the crashing report of a forty-five. He was down from his saddle, jerking his gun from holster, running for the protection of the huge cottonwood. The brown horse stood where he left him, head hanging, sides heaving.

Storm crouched behind the massive trunk. The advantage was Terrill's for the moment. Storm knew it was death to attempt a dash across the moonlit yard. He would be a target they couldn't miss.

The shot was troubling him. The bullet had not come his way. Jericho and Sooner must be somewhere close. He had told them to watch out for the girl. Something was wrong with the two cowboys or Fanny would not have screamed out her warning.

Voices in the patio garden broke the brief silence following the gunshot. Storm heard another sound. A woman's heartbroken sobs. Ynes, weeping!

A great fear suddenly racked Storm as he crouched there. Fanny was hurt. The shot had been for her. He had seen the sheriff's so-called deputies. Killers, in the pay of Ed Manners. They would have their secret instructions. Manners never intended that Fanny remain in the sheriff's hands for safe delivery to her mother. The drunken sheriff was only a cats-paw.

A sound behind him swung Storm's head in a brief look. Cacique, head drooping, was moving slowly toward the barn. Other eyes were watching the horse. Storm heard the sheriff's voice.

'Wonder where he holed up?' Terrill was obviously puzzled. 'Couldn't see him for dust when he lit from the saddle.'

'Only one place he could git to so quick.' Storm recognized French Jack's voice. 'I'm bettin' he made for the tree yonder.'

Storm judged the two men were close to the patio gate. He strained his ears. Their talk might prove profitable, decide his next move. Another voice reached him, sent a vast relief surging through him. Fanny's voice. She was comforting Ynes. Her words came with startling clearness. Storm suddenly realized her purpose. Fanny wanted him to hear, wanted to reassure him. Her coolness was a tonic to him. The sheriff was speaking again.

'Ain't likin' him so close to the rig, Frenchy. Left our rifles in the buckboard. Be hell if he gits hold of—'

'Don't talk so loud,' warned the other man in an angry whisper that cut through the night like a buzz-saw. 'Leave that bottle be, Vin. Gittin' drunker every minute.'

Storm guessed that Terrill was bolstering his courage with whiskey. He wasn't worrying much about the sheriff, though. French Jack was the one to look out for, and Jack's two companions.

'Ain't wantin' to stand here all night waitin' for him to show hisself.' Terrill's voice was blusteringly loud. He was suddenly shouting. 'Come away from that tree, MacKenzie. I got you spotted!' The gun in his hand sent out two quick bursts of flame and smoke.

Storm heard the vicious spat of a bullet on the rough bark of the tree, startled snorts came from the buckboard team tied to the hitch-rail. One of the horses squealed, began to plunge frantically. The tie-rope snapped, and as the front wheels cramped under the backward push, the rear end spun around, almost pinned Storm against the tree.

A rifle leaned on the back seat. Storm made a lightning grab, and as the frightened horses lunged away with the careening buckboard his fingers clasped the upended barrel and jerked the rifle over the spinning wheel.

Angry shouts rose from the patio gate. Storm glimpsed a man running into the yard, recognized French Jack, evidently bent on halting the runaway team before the buckboard was completely wrecked. French Jack must have momentarily forgotten Storm in the excitement.

Storm stepped from behind the tree with the rifle, coolly put his sights on the running man, and pulled the trigger. Frenchy never knew what hit him. He was suddenly down on his face. Dust drifted, hid him from view.

The crashing report of the rifle seemed to bewilder the whiskey-befuddled Terrill. He started to run toward the fallen man, apparently suddenly realized it was a bullet from Storm's rifle that had dropped his deputy. Heedless of the runaway team he swung in an abrupt turn in the direction of the gate. He stumbled, went sprawling in front of the runaways, now circling back in panic-stricken flight. There was a screech from the sheriff as the careening buckboard passed over him.

Storm restrained the impulse to run to the man. Two more of the deputies were still somewhere in the patio garden. He was in a killing mood at that moment. He wanted to get the sights of his rifle on them, blot them from life as he had blotted the life from French Jack. Storm was conscious of no pity for the man his bullet had just dropped in the dust. French Jack and his fellow-desperadoes had come to the ranch bent on murder.

The runaways found the wide-open gate, went tearing down the avenue with the wildly careening buckboard. A man's voice lifted in a shout from the patio. 'Hey, Frenchy! What's goin' on out there?'

The man repeated his question, voice hoarse with growing fear and bewilderment. He could not be sure just what had taken place in the yard. 'Looks like MacKenzie grabbed the team an' beat it away from here.'

The man came running down the patio walk, booted feet making a loud clatter on the flagstones. Clouds suddenly veiled the moon, shadowed the yard. Storm saw a vague shape appear from the patio gate, heard a startled grunt, a loud shout.

'Hell's busted loose here, Slim! Looks like MacKenzie got Frenchy and the sheriff when he grabbed the buckboard. Both of 'em layin' here in the yard.'

There was a silence, and then the other man's worried voice: 'I ain't stayin' here, playin' nurse on this pair o' wildcats. I'm for gittin' away before MacKenzie heads back with help.'

Storm heard Fanny's voice. 'You've got the boys' guns,' she said coolly. 'They can't hurt you—if you want to go.'

'You bet I'm goin',' retorted the man. The sounds told Storm he was backing down the flag-stones, gun covering Jericho and Sooner.

The moon slid from under the cloud, washed the yard with silver again. The second man joined his companion at the garden gate. Both began running toward the avenue.

Storm dropped the rifle and drew his Colt. The men were in panic-stricken flight, but they would start shooting the moment they saw him. Storm wanted no more dead men in the ranch yard. He was willing to let them go.

They were running neck and neck, but several yards apart. It meant one of them would pass to the right, the other to the left of the tree. Storm real-ized there could be no dodging. They were bound to see him. He would be caught in a cross-fire.

Shouts, the clatter of running feet back at the house told him that Jericho and Sooner were making a quick dash into the hall for guns they knew would be in the rack. The cowboys were eager to square accounts.

One of the men, small, bowlegged, forged into the lead. He would pass to the right a split second ahead of his bigger, slower companion. Storm stepped out, the big tree covering him for the moment from the man approaching on the left. There was a startled grunt from the bowlegged runner, his gun flashed up. Storm's forty-five roared. He didn't wait to see the result of the shot.

He couldn't miss at that distance. The second man was past the tree. Red flame belched from his gun. An answering flame burst from Storm's forty-five, and suddenly there was a stillness in the yard.

Storm stood there, smoking gun in lowered hand. The thing had been too close, the thin line between life and death too dreadfully thin.

Somebody was racing down the long yard from the patio gate. Jericho, a rifle in his hands. He slid to a halt, stared at the two dead men, turned slowly and looked at Storm. He was puffing from the quick dash.

The cowboy's stricken face gave Storm the stimulus he needed. With an abrupt gesture he pushed the gun into holster. 'You never could run without losing your wind, Jericho.' There was a hint of bitter reproach in his voice. 'Those coyotes were too fast for you—and Sooner.'

Jericho gulped. For once he had no words. Storm took pity on him. 'There must have been some good reason,' he said. 'I'm not blaming you boys. Where's Sooner?'

'Sooner reckoned he'd stay with the women,' explained Jericho. 'We wasn't knowin' just what was goin' on out here in the yard. Them fellers beat it away, an' we heard the shootin'.'

Storm's smile was grimly approving. 'Sooner did right, staying with the women. You, too, Jericho. You didn't know what you'd run into out here, but you came on the run.'

'Would have come quicker.' Jericho's tone was embarrassed. 'Had to get me a gun from the hall.' He shook his head ruefully. 'Them fellers got the drop on Sooner an' me, boss . . . took our guns.'

'I'm not blaming you,' repeated Storm. 'Terrill was sheriff. . . . You wouldn't guess what he was up to.'

'Sooner an' me wouldn't have let him take her,' asserted the cowboy. 'We'd have had Terrill an' his bunch on the run if Ynes hadn't busted into the thing.'

'Ynes?' Storm's brows lifted inquiringly.

Jericho gave a brief account of the part played by Ynes. They were close to the patio gate now. 'Miss Winston was scared they'd kill Ynes. . . . Nothin' for us to do but let 'em take our guns.'

'Nothing else you could do,' agreed Storm. He halted, stared at the twisted heap lying in the dust. 'Terrill's dead,' he added. 'Head's crushed like an eggshell.' He pushed through the gate, in haste to see Fanny. The dead men could wait.

Jericho followed him up the flagstones. Somebody had lit the hall lamp. Fanny was standing in the wide entrance, eagerly watching his approach. Storm came to an abrupt standstill. He was suddenly looking back down the years, a vivid picture of his mother framed in the same doorway, watching his father and himself coming up the walk. They had been gone for a week on the spring roundup. Storm was remembering how his father had halted his stride and looked at the woman waiting in the soft lamplight. His mother was wearing a new dress of soft pale green with low-cut bodice and many ruffles. The same dress was on the girl now standing in the old ranch-house hall.

Perhaps Fanny divined his thoughts, memories aroused by the sight of her in his mother's dress. She moved slowly toward him, met him on the steps, gave him her hands.

'I was sure you would come, Storm'—it was the first time she had used his name. To hear it on her lips made him tingle. 'I knew that man lied when he said you were in—in jail.'

'I got out,' Storm said briefly.

'Of course you would.' There was pride in the simple statement. She looked at him intently. 'You're dreadfully tired.' She faltered, eyes suddenly wet.

'It's done with,' Storm comforted. 'Nobody is going to harm you. We won't let anybody harm you.'

Ynes was suddenly padding from the hall, eyes wet with tears, arms reaching out to him. '*Stormito mio! Ave Maria Purisima!* Thank the Good God you have safely come to us! Alas, I did lose my head when those men tried to drag our little lamb away!'

Storm kissed her, patted her hands. He was glad Fanny did not understand Spanish, might be embarrassed to know she was their little lamb. He was still more thankful as the excited Ynes continued her torrent of words.

'Ah, *Stormito mio*—she is the flower I would have you pick for this house. I knew my many prayers were answered when you brought her here. She is your mother over again, so beautiful, so sweet a soul!'

'Hush, hush,' Storm told her in Spanish. 'You must not say foolish things.' He caught Jericho and Sooner exchanging amused looks. They knew enough Spanish to understand.

Ynes gave him a wise smile. 'Not foolish things, Stormito. Do not pretend with me who was the first to hold you in my arms and show you to your father—here on this very same veranda.' She turned back to the door. 'Tomasa is preparing good food. We will eat, all of us, and be happy.' Her smile went to Sooner and Jericho. *'Arroz con pollo,'* she added invitingly.

Storm shook his head. 'We have things to do, Ynes. Later, perhaps.' He gave the girl a brief smile. 'Later,' he repeated.

Sooner Bass and Jericho followed him down the walk. They knew what Storm meant. Dead men were lying in the yard.

Fanny watched until the patio gate closed them from view, then went slowly into the house. She was thinking too, about those dead men. She was thinking how different it might have been. It might have been Storm MacKenzie, lying out there.

21
The Diamond M Prepares for War

CLOUDS were piling above the distant San Franciscos when Storm came out from his breakfast. He watched them for a few moments, fingers busy with cigarette paper and tobacco. Rain coming, according to the old tradition. If not today, tomorrow. Storm hoped it would hold off until tomorrow. Not that rain would be unwelcome: the range could stand a good soaking. Storm snapped a match across thumbnail and lit his cigarette. Rain or no rain, it promised to be quite a day. His plans were well laid.

He lowered himself into the manzanita chair. The sky was still blue above the dark slopes of the Palos Verdes. Storm's brow wore a hint of a frown as he looked across at the low wooded hills. Diamond M range, now, but he had bought himself a lot of trouble when he made that deal with old Ben Hendricks. He'd been on the jump ever since, what with dodging bushwhackers and rescuing a girl from assassins who wanted to kill her because she had chanced to learn of a plot against himself and the ranch.

There were compensations. The Palos Verdes deal was responsible for bringing things to a head. Rain would probably be falling before the day was done, but the setting sun would see a rainbow in the sky, a rainbow of promise of better days to come.

A man hurried in from the patio gate, spurs rasping the flagstones as he clattered up to the veranda.

'*Buenos dias*, boss.' High Hat sank down on the top step, folded arms resting on doubled-up knees.

'When did *you* get in?' Storm looked at him in surprise.

'Jim Race was some worried, missin' you last night back in town.' High Hat's wide mouth twisted in an ironical smile. 'Jim's actin' as nervous as a settin' hen,' he confided.

'Had some trouble last night,' Storm explained.

High Hat nodded, fished a plug of tobacco and gnawed reflectively. 'Was hearin' about it from the boys when I got in from the camp. You'd gone to bed, but Sooner an' Jericho was still chewin' the rag over in the bunkhouse.'

'Jim send any special word?' Storm was suddenly anxious.

'Naw.' High Hat replaced the plug of tobacco in his shirt pocket. 'Jim was only wantin' some word 'bout *you*. Didn't know but what somethin' had put a crimp in this War Dance bus'ness.'

'Nothing's been changed,' Storm assured the cowboy. 'Better get your breakfast, High Hat. We'll be starting as soon as Pete Kendall and Yuma get here.'

'You bet!' High Hat got to his feet. 'Mebbe my last breakfast, huh. Reckon I'll fill up good. Hope

Tomasa has plenty flapjacks. Can eat a stack of 'em, way my stummick's rattlin' ag'in my backbone.' He vanished around the house.

A wagon rattled into the yard, drew up near the barn, and presently Jericho and Sooner pushed through the side gate.

'Planted 'em down in Coyote Gulch,' Sooner Bass said in response to Storm's questioning look. 'Miguel has already headed for town with the sheriff. Miguel's got the story fixed up good.'

'Get your breakfasts, boys,' Storm said, after a brief silence. 'We're starting as quick as Kendall and Yuma get in. High Hat's inside,' he added slyly. 'Says he's got a lot of room for breakfast.'

'The long-legged old buzzard,' grumbled Jericho. 'Ain't never seen High Hat when he wasn't cravin' food. Come on, Sooner—he'll be eatin' that table bare!'

Fanny came out, and stood leaning against the Diamond M post. She wore a cotton print dress, a rose-pink thing with elbow sleeves. Ynes had been digging deep into the old trunks. Storm felt pleased.

Fanny guessed his thoughts. 'I feel a bit quaint, but I'm awfully glad to have something to wear.' She changed the subject abruptly. 'I've been dying to know why Jericho is—*Jericho*. It can't be his *real* name.'

Storm chuckled. 'Don't you ever call him Jeremiah. He won't like it.'

221

'Jeremiah!' Fanny laughed. 'Why not call him plain *Jerry?*'

'Because his last name happens to be Coe,' Storm informed her. 'Jeremiah Coe just couldn't be anything but Jericho.'

'I suppose not,' agreed Fanny. 'It's what they call a natural.' Her face sobered. 'I heard what Sooner said to you—about those men.'

'I'm sorry.' His voice was curt. 'You mustn't think about it.'

'I can't help thinking about it.' Her eyes darkened with anxiety. 'What can you say to—to people?'

'I'm saying nothing. Nobody is going to waste time wondering about them.'

'Ed Manners will,' the girl said in a troubled voice. '*He'll* be wondering.'

'He'll keep his wondering to himself,' said Storm. 'Ed Manners isn't one to involve himself. He'll wonder, but he won't talk, especially now that Terrill is dead. Terrill won't be able to tell him anything.'

'Sooner said Miguel is taking the sheriff back to town,' Fanny reminded. 'People will want to know how he met his death.'

'Miguel is telling them exactly what took place. The sheriff was drunk, got mangled to death under the wheels of his buckboard.' Storm shrugged his shoulders. 'Terrill was a sot. It's known all over the county that he was seldom sober.'

'I'm not criticizing,' Fanny said in a low voice. 'It's because I'm afraid for—for you.'

'You needn't be.' His face darkened. 'What good will it do, telling anybody about those dead men? Nobody cares what's become of them. They were killers, gallows-birds.'

'I'm sorry. Please forgive me for—for talking about it.'

'You think I'm callous—making myself the law,' Storm said harshly.

'No—no!' Fanny spoke pleadingly. 'It's not true!'

'I'll tell you this much,' Storm went on more gently, 'when the law is back in this county, the law will have the full story from me about those dead men. I won't be afraid to tell the truth, say that I shot them to save my life—and yours.' He spoke quietly, but his words had an edge to them. 'What else could I do? A man doesn't stop to argue when wolves are leaping at his throat.'

Fanny's eyes widened. She was remembering something. 'Why—that's exactly what Mr. Stagg said when—' She broke off, face suddenly aflame. She couldn't very well tell him about her talk with Dave Stagg.

Storm was speaking again. 'I hate this killing,' he said bitterly. 'But what could I do?'

'You did right,' Fanny declared with sudden vehemence. 'I'm glad you shot those men. I'd have done the same—yes, I would!'

'You've been very brave,' Storm said in a low voice. 'You saved my life. I heard you calling out to me just as Cacique took the jump over the fence.'

'I didn't know I was screaming until I heard my own voice,' Fanny confessed honestly. 'I could have died,' she added.

Her fingers were playing with the mark made by the branding iron. She turned and looked at it, smiled over her shoulder. 'Ynes was telling me the story. Your mother must have been wonderful.'

'There're times when you make me think of her.' Storm's voice deepened. 'Gave me a start when I saw you in the hall last night, the lamplight in your hair—that dress.'

Fanny hastily changed the subject. 'I'm worried about Mother. The sheriff said she had sent him.'

'Manners put her up to it.'

'I'm sure of that. The whole affair was a trick.' The girl's voice was unsteady. 'Manners knows that I can make trouble for him. He—he won't rest until I'm—'

'He'll never have another chance,' Storm said.

There was a silence, broken by the rattle of buckboard wheels. Storm got out of his chair. 'Pete Kendall—and Yuma.' He looked at Fanny, then quickly shifted his gaze toward the corral. 'I'm leaving with the boys in a few minutes.'

'You'll be gone—long?' Her voice was low.

'We'll be back by night,' he answered, not meeting her look.

'I wasn't fooled,' Fanny said. 'I knew why Sooner and Jericho stayed so close to the house. You were afraid there'd be trouble.'

'Manners won't be trying again, not so soon.' Storm was halfway down the steps. 'If things go right today he won't trouble you—or me, ever again.'

'Storm'—the girl's low voice faltered—'I know where you are going—'

He looked back at her, his face grim.

'Please—please be careful—' She was suddenly running into the hall.

Storm stood there for a long moment, his look following her, then he went slowly down the flagged walk.

He was surprised to see Dave Stagg climbing from the buckboard. The old liveryman chuckled at the look on his face. 'Figgered I'd come along with Pete an' Yuma. Kind of cravin' some action. Looks like we'll git plenty over on War Dance.'

Pete Kendall's choleric face seemed even redder than usual. He was helping Yuma extract two Winchester rifles from under the front seat.

'Hello, Stormy. Brought our guns along. Reckon you'll fix us up with horses.'

'Saddled and waiting,' assured Storm. He stared suspiciously at Dave Stagg. 'You're keeping something back,' he accused. 'You didn't come out just for a chance to pot a few cattle-rustlers.'

'You're too doggone smart, Stormy,' grumbled

the veteran ex-freighter. 'Cain't I renoo my hell-bustin' youth with some rustler-skelpin'?'

High Hat, followed by Jericho and Sooner, came with quick choppy strides from the patio gate. Yuma waved his rifle in answer to their welcoming shouts. 'Reckon I'll go take a look at our broncs, boss,' he said to Pete Kendall. He went loping across the yard to overtake the Diamond M men. Kendall looked at Storm. His face was grave.

'Dave an' me's been some worried, Stormy. Ain't got the straight of it—about what happened last night.'

'Stormy acts like he don't want to talk,' Dave Stagg commented. 'Lookin' him over from head to foot, I'd say he's still all in one piece.'

'What have you heard—about last night?' said Storm. 'I'm hoping it's very little,' he added pointedly, 'and I'm hoping it goes no further.'

'You can count on us, Stormy,' reassured Dave. 'Cain't blame us for bein' worried.'

'Let's have the worst first,' Storm begged.

'It's my notion this Ducker feller's plumb out of his head,' Dave went on. 'Claims you was in jail—a prisoner—an' that you throwed a lamp at him an' set him afire.'

The two men were watching Storm closely. He shook his head. 'You must be right about this Ducker being crazy, Dave. What would I be doing in a jail?' His eyes twinkled amusement. 'Anybody else but this Ducker saying things?'

226

'Nary a word from nobody,' assured Dave. 'Reckon Ducker is sure crazy. Probably was drunk an' set hisself afire. Won't see out of one of his eyes no more.'

'What's the talk about the sheriff?'

'No talk a-tall. Miguel was cartin' him into town when we come along. Reckon there's plenty folks doin' some wonderin' right now, though.'

'Miguel said the buckboard had run over him,' put in Pete Kendall. 'Don't surprise me none—the way Terrill was always soused.'

'Be a nine days' wonder,' commented Dave. His keen eyes bored at Storm, but whatever his private thoughts he was keeping them to himself. 'You'll be the next sheriff, Stormy. We're goin' to give the Little Mesalta a chance to be decent ag'in.'

'Not on your life,' laughed Stormy. 'No sheriffing for me.' He was suddenly thoughtful. 'Jim Race is the man for you. Jim's just naturally born to be a sheriff.'

'Jim Race,' agreed Dave. 'Stormy—we just got to git out an' elect him. Be a walk-over, once we tie a can to Ed Manners.'

Storm suddenly remembered something. 'What about the Pinkerton man?' he queried.

'Fred Morton didn't get in yet,' replied Kendall disappointedly. 'Be in on the afternoon stage, most likely.'

'I'm hoping he's right,' Storm said feelingly.

'The boys have got the horses ready,' observed

the Lazy K man. He dragged a holster and gun from the buckboard and began buckling the belt around his hips. 'I'll mosey over an' size up that horse you picked out for me.' He hurried away.

Dave looked at Storm, a hint of reproach in his one eye. 'There's a lot you ain't tellin', Stormy. Never knowed you to be so close-mouthed.'

'It's for the best.' Storm's curt rejoinder was softened by his warm smile.

'I savvy.' Dave nodded soberly. 'I'm with you all the way, son.'

'I'll tell you about it, some day,' Storm promised.

'Don't need to,' drawled the old man. 'You're Jim MacKenzie's boy, an' that's enough for me.' He turned abruptly to lighter matters, secretly disturbed by the hint of pain in Storm's eyes. 'Got news that'll make your eyes pop. Louella's goin' to marry A. Solem.'

Storm blinked at him. 'Say that again!' he pleaded. 'Something wrong with my ears.'

'I said Louella is goin' to marry A. Solem,' chuckled Dave. 'Was goin' to tell you about it last evenin', but Burl Jenners's comin' with his story about Ed Manners an' the Pinkerton feller clean drove it from my mind.'

'Burl still in town?' asked Storm.

'Sure. Burl ain't leavin' till Morton gits here an' settles this Manners bus'ness. Well, about Louella. . . . Seems she went after Solem like a clawin' wildcat for lettin' her grandpa turn all that money over to you, used her nails on his face an' kicked his shins good. A. Solem got awful peevish . . . took the gal over his knee and sure spanked her good an' plenty.'

'Fine for A. Solem,' laughed Storm. 'Didn't know it was in him.'

'Ben was there in the store, saw the whole play. Ben says Louella was one awful surprised gal. She got up an' looked at Solem like she'd never seen him before, begun to cry an' say she'd been the doggonedest fool ever was born. Ben says he told A. Solem the spankin' was the best thing ever happened to Louella. Was kickin' hisself for not doin' it on his own account.'

'Where does this wedding business come in?' Storm wanted to know in a bewildered voice.

Dave chuckled. 'Well, when A. Solem seen her bawlin' he plumped down on his knees like he was prayin' to her, says lot o' funny things, like she was his star an' precious jewel an' that he was lovin' her like mad. Reckon it got Louella to thinkin' hard. Ben says she stood there starin' 'round the store, kind o' cool an' thoughtful, like she was thinkin' *awful* hard. Fust thing he knew, Ben says, she had her arms 'round A. Solem's neck an' was kissin' him, tellin' him he was the fust man that had sense enough to know she was worth a good lickin'.' Dave paused, looked at Storm thoughtfully. 'Ben says he'll be after you for that money . . . wants to give it for a weddin' present. It's goin' into the bus'ness, A. Solem says.'

'I sent that money over to the bank in Phoenix,' Storm told him. 'It's darn good news, Dave. I kind of liked that girl. Got a lot of good in her, and A. Solem will make her a grand husband. What's more, he'll be a rich husband.'

'I've a notion that's what Louella was thinkin',' chuckled the old man.

They joined the waiting group at the corral and swung up to their saddles. Storm failed to see Fanny Winston watching from the patio gate as they rode out of the yard.

She stood there, eyes fixed on the trailing dust until the haze melted into the distance. Then she went slowly up the path and around the house into the big garden in the back. There would be restful peace there, under the tall whispering pines. She wanted to think of Storm MacKenzie—pray for his safe return.

22
The Fight on War Dance

THE cattle drifted into the stone corral from two directions. The bawling herd pushing up between high red cliffs from the lower gap showed signs of weariness. It was a hard drive from the cedar brakes country. Yipping yells of cowboys harrying the laggard rear guard rose shrilly from the distance.

The second herd was moving down from the higher reaches of Wild Horse Flats. They romped through the upper gap, some two hundred or more bellowing steers. The grass was plentiful up on the flats, but they were remembering the old stamping grounds down in the cedar brakes and were of a mind to get there as fast as four legs could carry them. The first arrivals, now choking the bottle-neck, formed an impassable barrier of tossing horned heads. In a few minutes the two lines of cattle became one restlessly milling herd. Riders appeared at the upper and lower gaps, quickly dragged strands of barbed wire across the openings, swung back into saddles and disappeared.

Eyes were watching from the War Dance cliffs. 'Don't savvy this play,' Red Yessap muttered to the bearded man who crouched by his side behind the split boulder that overhung the cliff. 'Where in hell's the outfit? Why ain't they showin' up?'

'Search me,' grunted Vordal. 'At that I'd say Ed sent us the right tip. Them cows down there proves he got it straight from Jim Race. Jim was in the bar, drinkin', let out they was cuttin' the cows today for the Jenners shipment.'

Yessap was not satisfied. 'Them fellers that strung up the wires has gone,' he said. 'I ain't likin' this, Vordal.'

'No sense you gittin' jumpy,' growled the bearded man. 'We got a set-up as cain't go wrong.' His hand caressed the stock of his rifle. 'The outfit'll be ridin' in, you can bet. What else for is the cows here? Reckon they're waitin' for MacKenzie. He mebbe figgers to do the cuttin'.'

'I sure crave to git my sights on him,' muttered Yessap.

Vordal patted his rifle stock again. 'Be like pottin' rabbits!'

'Ain't likin' it,' grumbled Yessap. He got to his feet. Another man lay sprawled behind a boulder several yards away. He grinned as he met the outlaw leader's morose look.

'Seems like them Diamond M fellers is lost some place, Red.'

Yessap dropped an oath, moved slowly along the rimrock. His anxiety was fast growing into a panic. The signs all indicated that the tip from Ed Manners was correct. The milling herd in the stone corral below was there for a purpose. Cattle were not gathered off the range for the fun of it. Yessap didn't like the look of things. He smelled trouble.

His inspection satisfied him that the members of his gang were all at their stations. Vordal's Red Torchers, too. Yessap had rebelled at having to share the profits with Vordal's men. He was suspicious of Ed's insistence on having the Red Torchers mixed up in the affair. It was back in the rustler's mind that Manners planned some treachery. He had noticed Vordal's sly looks.

Red Yessap's thin lips twisted in a wicked smile. Two could play the double-crossing game. He'd rope Vordal's body to his own saddle, ship him back to Ed Manners. He'd carve a bloody double cross on Vordal's back for Manners to see and understand.

The rustler made his way back to the big split rock. He'd wait awhile. No sense going off half-cock. The Diamond M outfit must be somewhere close. Any moment might see MacKenzie and his riders pushing into the stone corral. Good pickings, when the thing was done. Close to a thousand head down there, a good half of them prime steers. Yessap's eyes gleamed. No sense making a divvy with Ed Manners. He knew where to get a good price for stolen cows.

Vordal grinned at him as he crouched down under the split boulder. 'You're sure jumpy,' he sneered. He broke off. The curious light in the outlaw leader's pale slate eyes made him uneasy. He forced a laugh. 'Hell—you sure can look mean—poison mean—when you git scary.'

'Scared nothin',' grunted Yessap. He cocked an eye up at the sun. 'Mos' noon. . . . Reckon I'll send word up to Tonto. He'll be wonderin' what keeps our guns quiet. The cows is makin' plenty noise for him to know they've got here. Tonto won't savvy we're still waitin' for the outfit to show up.'

Tonto was not wondering. He was sitting against a rock, his ankles bound, his hands tied behind his back, and his own soiled bandanna effectively preventing him from giving vocal expression to his outraged feelings.

Storm was counting the horses tied to various piñon trees. 'Fourteen,' he said to Jim Race.

'One of 'em here.' Jim looked at the unfortunate Tonto. 'That makes thirteen more of the coyotes down on the War Dance cliffs some place. Mebbe more of 'em hidin' out at the gaps,' he added thoughtfully.

'Mebbe this bat-eared jasper'll tell us,' Sooner Bass suggested. He stared hard at Tonto. 'Reckon he'd sooner talk than swing.' His glance went significantly to one of the larger piñons. 'He ain't so heavy but what he'd dangle good from that tree.'

Storm nodded, Jericho loosened the bandanna. Sooner poked his gun against the man's ribs. 'How about it, mister? Any more of you polecats holed up in the War Dance?'

Tonto shook his head. There were no men posted at the gaps. Red hadn't thought it necessary.

'If you're lyin', we'll swing you sure,' promised Sooner Bass. 'I'd sooner swing a damn rustler than eat.'

Jericho retied the bandanna, announced he was 'r'arin' to go.'

'Sooner we git this bus'ness done the sooner we can eat,' High Hat said. 'Speakin' plumb personal, I'd sooner eat than swing any damn rustler.'

'You shut up!' Sooner Bass glared at him. 'Here's Yuma,' he added.

The Lazy K man hurried up, rifle in hand, eyes bright with excitement. 'Got 'em all spotted,' he announced. 'Yessap's down there with Vordal, holed up ag'in a big chimney rock. A couple more of 'em are layin' ten yards up in a bunch of scrub, an' I counted seven of the skunks hid down on a ledge that shelves out from the cliff. Big clump of manzanita covers 'em from anybody lookin' up their way from the corral.'

'Good work,' praised Storm. He smiled at Pete Kendall. 'Any time you want to fire Yuma he's got a job on the Diamond M payroll.'

'Over my dead body,' snapped the owner of the Lazy K. 'Yuma's the best damn trailer in the territory. You ain't talkin' him away from me, Stormy.'

Dave Stagg, leaning on an ancient Sharps buffalo gun, said thoughtfully, 'Four an' seven makes eleven . . . leavin' two more Yuma ain't spotted.'

'Eight of us,' Jim Race enumerated, 'not countin' the rest o' the boys outside the gaps. Reckon they'll take care of any strays.'

Storm nodded. 'All right, let's get moving,' he said tersely. He hesitated, looked at Dave Stagg. 'Somebody should stay here with these horses.'

The old ex-freighter glared at him. 'Ain't carin' for the way you look at me, Stormy.'

'We don't want any of them to make a break for the horses—get away,' Storm rejoined.

'What for you pickin' on me?' grumbled Dave. 'Ain't fired off this old Sharps for a coon's age. Kind o' hanker to hear her roar ag'in.'

'Bet that old meat-in-the-pot kicks worse'n any mule,' gibed Jericho.

Dave fixed him with a stern eye. 'She's a man's weepon, sonny. When you git growed I'll mebbe let you try her out.'

'I'd sooner shoot off a cannon,' disparaged Sooner Bass.

Dave snorted indignantly. 'All right, Stormy. I'm settin' here an' ride herd on the broncs. I'll likely spoil the huntin' if I go down there with them squirtgun-totin' yearlin's.'

They were suddenly gone from sight, making their way with Indian stealth through the growth of scrubby piñons. Storm followed the faint tracks that he knew led to the big chimney rock. He wanted Red Yessap, and he'd a score to settle with Vordal.

Pete Kendall, with Yuma, High Hat, and Jim Race, made for the overhanging ledge. Jericho and Sooner said they would take care of the four men lying in ambush near Yessap's chimney rock. There would be two more rustlers Yuma had failed to locate. It was possible Yessap had posted them as lookouts. The thought worried Storm. The rustlers outnumbered them. Thirteen of them to seven, not counting Dave Stagg left on guard with the horses. Chance discovery by the lookouts would weaken the advantage of surprise.

A bullet screamed past his head. Storm threw himself prone behind a low boulder, listened with dismay to the crashing report of the rifle reverberating between the cliffs. No surprise now. The lookouts had warned Yessap.

He crawled forward, slid down a sheer overhang of rock, and flattened behind another boulder. He could see Yessap, crouching in the scrub. Vordal was not visible.

Another rifle shot blasted the silence, sent echoes rolling between the lofty canyon walls. It came from the direction taken by Pete Kendall's party. Almost instantly an answering fusillade roared and crashed into fading echoes.

Storm gave his attention to the man crouching in the scrub near the chimney rock. He wanted the outlaw alive. He was sick of killing.

Rifles were crashing just above him. Sooner and Jericho, at grips with the four rustlers they had picked for themselves. A yell of pain lifted shrilly above the thundering gunshots. A rustler down.

A man's face peered from behind the chimney rock. Vordal's bearded face. Suddenly he was out on the ledge, skylined against the opposite cliffs. His rifle swung up point blank at Storm, fell suddenly from his grasp as a gun roared from somewhere in the higher ridge behind. Dave Stagg's ancient Sharps.

Storm saw Vordal spin around as though struck by a bolt of lightning. The next instant he disappeared headlong into the chasm below.

Something else caught Storm's eyes, momentarily distracted by the spectacular end to Vordal.

Yessap, streaking away from the scrub, making for a maze of sawtooth rocks. Storm fired, saw the outlaw stumble, go down on one knee. Storm ran toward him. Yessap twisted over on his side, hand jerking at a holster gun. Storm flattened behind the cover of a nearby upthrust of jagged rock.

'I've got you, Yessap.' Storm's voice lifted just enough to carry.

'Yeah?' The outlaw's voice was defiant. 'Why don't you come an' git me?'

'Your leg's broken,' Storm said. 'No chance for you to get away.'

'Show your head an' I'll blow it to hell,' invited Yessap coolly. There was nothing yellow in the little desperado's makeup.

Storm's eyes narrowed. Yessap would shoot the instant a target was offered. The man was notoriously fast with a gun. Storm knew he wouldn't miss at that close range. He reached out for a piece of broken piñon branch blown down the hill by the wind, took off his hat and put it on top of the stick. An old trick, but there was a chance Yessap would fall for it. The man was desperate, his trigger-finger nervous.

Storm slowly raised the hat until the crown hovered between two of the jagged pinnacles. Instantly five shots roared out, almost faster than he could count them. For the moment Yessap was harmless, his gun empty. Storm sprang to his feet, leveled his rifle.

'Good shooting, Yessap.' He toed at his fallen hat. 'Lucky for me my head wasn't inside that Stetson.'

Yessap cursed, hurled his empty gun at him. 'I wish Ed Manners's head had been under that hat,' he said viciously.

'You've ruined a good hat,' chuckled Storm. 'Worth the price, though, Yessap.'

The outlaw cursed him. 'You've been too smart for me—too smart for Ed Manners.'

'Where does Ed come in?' asked Storm softly.

'He fixed up this job for me,' answered the rustler.

'Talk some more,' encouraged Storm. 'Might be good for you.'

'Go to hell,' muttered Yessap, and then, thoughtfully, 'What you want to know?'

'What do you know about the Red Torchers?'

'Plenty, an' Ed Manners knows more'n I do.'

'What do you mean by that?' asked Storm.

'The Red Torch gang is Ed's little scheme for scarin' fellers into sellin' out their timberland to him. Ed turns the stuff over to the Great Western.' Yessap rapped out an oath. 'Wasn't in my line, so Ed had Vordal run the show for him.'

'Warde mixed up in this business—the Red Torchers, I mean?' Storm flung the question harshly. His rage was mounting.

'Not that I know of,' replied the outlaw sullenly. 'Reckon Warde wasn't knowin' the way Ed framed fellers like Tim Shale an' Ben Hendricks. Warde wasn't wantin' to know too much. He's a feller that likes to git what he's after an' no questions asked.' Yessap stifled a groan. 'My leg's sure broke—an' hurtin' like hell,' he added.

A stillness had settled over the War Dance, broken only by the ceaseless bawling of the restless cattle in the stone corral below. Storm strained his ears, caught the sound of voices. Jericho and Sooner suddenly pushed through the scrub, herding two sullen-faced prisoners.

'Looks like the shindig's over, boss.' Jericho's voice was jubilant.

Storm looked sharply at Sooner. The cowboy's wrist wore a bandage—his bandanna.

Sooner sent him a rueful smile. 'The other two fellers got worse,' he said grimly. 'We left 'em layin' for the buzzards.'

Somebody was shouting. Pete Kendall's harsh voice. 'Got our bunch hog-tied, Stormy, all that's left of 'em. How's things your way?'

'Everything fine, Pete. Send High Hat over. Need help to carry Yessap up the hill. Red's got a broken leg.'

There was a silence, then Jim Race's voice, unnaturally solemn. 'Cain't send High Hat, Stormy. I'll be right over myself.'

Jericho and Sooner exchanged startled looks, darted quick glances at Storm. His gaze was fixed on the wounded outlaw.

'I should kill you, Yessap.' Storm spoke huskily. 'I should kill you—but I'm sick of killing, even worthless scum like you.'

Jim Race came plowing through the scrub. The foreman's seamed, leathery face looked old and worn. 'Got bad news, Stormy—' His voice broke.

Storm nodded. 'High Hat?'

'He caught a bullet,' Jim said. 'Yeah—High Hat's done for, Stormy.'

Storm drew a long breath. 'High Hat said something queer this morning—said he was maybe eating his last breakfast and hoped there'd be plenty of flapjacks.'

'High Hat always went strong on flapjacks,' Jericho said mournfully. 'Johnnycake used to ride him for always callin' for more flapjacks.'

They stared at each other, their hearts heavy. Words were useless. They all knew High Hat— knew he was *a man.*

Jim Race and Storm picked up the wounded Yessap and started up the hill. Dave Stagg gave them a sharp look. Something was wrong. He hadn't heard about High Hat yet.

Storm said briefly: 'Much obliged for that shot, Dave. Vordal had the drop on me.'

The veteran ex-freighter grunted a protest. 'Ain't needin' thanks for exterminatin' a skunk. I got me a skelp back in the hotel, took from an Injun as was a damsite better man than Vordal.' Dave scowled. 'Wasn't likin' the notion of him pottin' you,

Stormy—nor what he tried to do to the Winston gal.'

Storm left the prisoners with Jim Race. Only nine of the rustlers had survived the fight, several of them badly wounded.

'Jericho and Sooner will take High Hat back to the ranch,' Storm decided. 'There's a place for him in the garden.'

'What'll I do with this bunch o' cow thieves?' Jim wanted to know.

Something in his voice brought a stern look from Storm. 'No necktie party,' he warned. 'You bring them into town and jail them.'

'Huh!' Jim's voice was glum. 'Just as you say.'

'We're having you appointed sheriff for Terrill's unexpired term,' Storm told him. 'Next election you'll be sheriff of this county.'

'You're the boss,' Jim Race said simply.

Pete Kendall and Dave Stagg were already in their saddles. Jim swung up to his horse and the three men started down the trail, faces grim with resolute purpose. They had a job of work waiting for them in Mesalta.

23
Storm MacKenzie Rides

BURL JENNERS was waiting in front of the livery barn when they rode in. 'Saw your dust liftin' over the ridge.' He indicated a long, lean man sprawled in Dave's chair. 'Fred Morton just got in. Missed the stage yesterday and hired a rig in Flagstaff.'

The Pinkerton man got out of his chair, acknowledged their greetings with a curt nod. He had watchful eyes under drooping lids.

Storm said brusquely, 'Let's get it over with.' He looked at Morton. 'Will you be sure of your man when you see him?'

'Never forget a face.' The Pinkerton man smiled. 'Would know Ed Mertz anywhere.'

'Won't matter much if you're wrong about him,' Storm continued. 'We have enough on Ed Manners to hang him.'

'I'm not weeping,' retorted Morton.

'I'm charging Ed Manners with cattle-stealing, attempted kidnapping, extortion, conspiracy to defraud—and *murder*.' Storm looked at his friends. 'Am I right?'

'Right as rain,' grunted Pete Kendall.

Dave Stagg nodded. 'I can hear Ed's neck crackin',' he drawled.

'I'm wasting my time here,' grumbled Morton. 'I'm in this town looking for a forger. You've got me beat with a murder charge.'

'You're not running out on us, Morton,' Storm said good-naturedly. 'If Manners *is* your forger we want to know. Will help clear up a few puzzlers.'

'I'll mosey over to that funny bank of his and look him over,' agreed Morton.

'Keep your eyes peeled,' Dave called out softly. 'Ed may git the first look.'

The Pinkerton man glanced back at them. 'Always keep my eyes peeled,' he retorted. 'That's why I'm still on the job—hunting crooks.'

Storm waited until Morton was across the street. 'I think we'd better be close on his heels,' he said uneasily.

'My notion, too,' rejoined Dave Stagg.

'Come on!' exclaimed Burl Jenners. 'Fred don't know what he's gettin' into.'

They trooped over to the opposite sidewalk, Pete Kendall bringing up the rear. The Lazy K man was already dragging gun from holster.

Morton shook his head at them as they caught up with him in front of the bank. 'Nobody home,' he said.

'I'll go look in the bar,' offered Burl Jenners.

He was back in a few moments, his expression disappointed. 'Ed went off on his horse some place, from what the bartender says. Left less than an hour ago.'

They stared at each other, and Storm said thoughtfully, 'There's a side door, down in the alley.'

'What do you mean?' Morton stared at him.

'I'd like to have a look at his papers,' Storm said. 'I've my good reasons.'

'Let's try the side door,' agreed Morton dryly. 'I have proper authority.' He turned quickly into the alley. The others followed.

The side door was not locked. Manners must

have been in some haste when he left. The men walked in and down the passage to the front office. Morton halted, stared at the big oak desk, shook his head. 'No use looking in there.' His look shifted to the old-fashioned safe.

'Know how to open those things?' Storm spoke softly.

'I've done it before,' murmured the detective. 'This one looks easy.' He began twirling the dial and after a few attempts swung the door open. He looked around at Storm. 'What were you expecting to find?'

'A quitclaim deed to the Diamond M Ranch.'

Dave Stagg let out a startled grunt. 'The doggone skunk!'

Morton was fumbling in the drawers, finally drew out a folded document. He studied it intently, then gave Storm a curious look. 'Quitclaim deed from you to Ed Manners,' he said; 'makes him sole owner of the Diamond M Ranch and all you possess.'

Dave Stagg spoke again, voice choked with wrath. 'The crawlin' snake,' he muttered.

The Pinkerton detective smiled. 'Ed Mertz did this work.'

'I know I didn't.' Storm's tone was grim. 'I didn't make that signature.'

'Ed Mertz did it,' repeated Morton. 'I'd know his work anywhere.'

'Sure would fool me,' muttered Jenners. His face

wore an angry flush. 'Guess Manners is Mertz, all right.'

Morton nodded. 'Sure—sure. Couldn't be anybody else.' He was looking at Storm with puzzled eyes. 'Maybe you can tell us what this thing means.' He tapped the forged deed.

'Manners planned to have me murdered'—rage made Storm's voice tight. 'Yessap confessed,' he went on, looking at their aghast faces. 'Yessap was to get five thousand dollars and a half-cut in the cattle. Manners could have made that deed stand. It was known I'd borrowed money from him.'

There was a silence, broken by a growl from Pete Kendall. His choleric face was aflame. 'Let's go hunt him down—hang him to the first tree.'

'Don't blame you for feeling that way, mister.' Morton shook his head regretfully. 'I've a warrant for the arrest of Ed Mertz, alias Ed Manners. If lynching is the best you can think of, I'm sticking round till I get the handcuffs on him.'

Storm nodded agreement. 'Do that, Morton. He may show up in town any moment, and right now we have no sheriff handy.'

'I'll turn him over to you when you want him,' promised the detective.

'Somebody's tappin' on the window,' interrupted Burl Jenners.

Storm looked up, recognized Mrs. Winston. She crooked a beckoning finger at him.

'She wants you,' muttered Dave Stagg.

246

Storm nodded, went out to the street. Mrs. Winston gave him a frozen look.

'You dreadful creature!' Emotion took the breath from her. 'You—you vile kidnapper!'

'I'm not a kidnapper, Mrs. Winston. Your daughter is safe.' Storm kept his voice down. 'You'll know the truth soon—very soon.'

'You're not keeping her a minute longer at your miserable ranch. Lester Warde has gone to bring her home.'

Storm stared at her dumbfounded.

She saw his dismay, smiled triumphantly. 'Perhaps you don't know that my daughter is engaged to marry Lester Warde. They are very, very fond of each other. They'll be married immediately, just as quickly as we can get to Phoenix— and a minister.'

Storm hardly heard her.

'How long ago did Mr. Warde leave for the ranch?' He flung the question at her hoarsely.

Mrs. Winston took a backward step, frightened by his vehemence. 'Why'—she stammered— 'about an hour or two ago.' She was suddenly indignant again. 'It's none of your business. I was telling Mr. Manners Lester had gone for her. Mr. Manners said it was the only thing Lester could do.'

Mrs. Winston found herself talking to thin air. Storm was running across the street, dust spurting from boot-heels as he headed for the livery barn.

Cacique was still at the hitch-rail in front of the office. Storm grabbed the tie-rope loose, swung up into saddle, and in another moment the brown horse was running at top speed down the street.

24
Trial by Fire

THE long road followed the line of least resistance through a maze of canyons and gullies that yawned down from green-forested hills.

'We've crossed that creek four times,' Fanny Winston said to the man sitting by her side in the red-wheeled buggy.

'The Porcupine,' Lester Warde told her.

'Snake would make a better name,' Fanny declared.

'Already in use,' smiled the man. 'The Snake River—a big one.'

'The Little Snake, then; Little Snake Creek.' Fanny's light chatter was only a subterfuge, an attempt to smother growing doubts. She tried to push them aside. They came back at her, warning whispering voices. *You foolish girl. . . . You should not have come with this man. . . . You should not have come with Lester Warde. Foolish girl. . . . You're in for trouble. . . . What will Storm MacKenzie say when he finds you gone?* Fanny tried to shut them out. They refused to be shut out. Her head was aching miserably.

'Here's where we leave the Porcupine.' Warde's

voice broke into her reflections. He turned the team of bays off the dusty, bumpy road into a narrower road that was still more dusty and bumpy. Fanny saw that it went twisting up into pine-clad slopes.

'The Palos Verdes!' she exclaimed. She turned her face in a surprised look at him. 'Why do you want to go up there, Lester? The Palos Verdes belongs to the Diamond M Ranch.'

'MacKenzie won't own the Palos Verdes much longer.' Warde seemed amused. 'I hold his note for a lot of money with that timberland as security. Several miles longer to town by this road, but I want a look at things.'

'The Palos Verdes is Diamond M range!' Fanny found herself wondering at her vehemence. *The Diamond M—more than just a cattle brand. It was a symbol of two lives . . . of love and faith and courage.* 'Storm MacKenzie will never give up the Palos Verdes.'

The assertion visibly annoyed Warde. He muttered under his breath, flung her an exasperated look. 'I want that timber,' he said. 'I usually get what I want.'

'I don't see just how.' She was tingling. 'Storm says the Palos Verdes naturally belong to the Diamond M Ranch—like the nose on his face.'

'He's going to have his nose tweaked,' Warde told her grumpily. 'He won't be able to pay his note . . . Ed Manners guarantees he won't. I'll be logging that yellow pine inside of ninety days.'

'It's awfully cold!' Fanny was suddenly shivering. His mention of Ed Manners was like ice on her heart. *What did he mean?*

Warde's face came around in a surprised look. 'You're crazy. It's hot—blazing hot.' He was suddenly frowning. 'That haze up there looks like smoke.'

They drove along in silence, save for the steady beat of the horses' hoofs, the grind of the wheels as the buggy swayed and jolted up the steepening ascent. Fanny's thoughts went back to the moment of Lester Warde's appearance in the patio garden. She had just changed into the soft pale green dress, was sitting in Storm's big porch chair, her thoughts with him, wondering what was happening up on the War Dance trail. Storm had shown no sign of worry when he rode away with those men—only grim resolve to get something settled. Fanny was thinking, too, of Storm's mother, how she must have often waited on the veranda, perhaps in the same big manzanita chair, waiting for her husband's return from the dangerous adventures that were always a part of the pioneer ranchman's life. Storm's mother put on a new dress for his welcome, a dress of soft pale green—the one Fanny was wearing. She was feeling a little guilty about it, pretending something that would never be. She was conscious, too, of the curious look from Ynes as she passed through the hall, the Mexican woman's wise, knowing smile. Fanny felt she must explain to Ynes that she was practically engaged to marry Lester Warde.

And suddenly Lester Warde was approaching up the patio walk. He had come to take her back to town, he told her gravely. Her mother was prostrated with grief, was in danger of complete collapse, in fact was a very ill woman.

Fanny could find no argument to combat his resolve to carry her off to Mesalta—back to her mother. Lester was most final about it. She would be responsible if anything happened to her mother. There was a chance of a stroke . . . Mrs. Winston was in a bad way.

The narrow, twisting road leveled out across a stretch of flats covered with a growth of pine trees. Warde sent the bays along at a smart clip. Fanny glanced at him, was struck with the apprehensiveness in his eyes. She was suddenly aware, too, of heated waves of air blowing against her. She gave a startled little cry. The haze Lester had mentioned had deepened into billowing clouds of smoke.

'Lester!' Her tone was panicky.

'I thought we could make it across the ridge and down into the valley,' Warde said. 'Wasn't expecting the wind to change. Blowing harder, too.'

'We can't go on,' Fanny declared. 'Look at it! We can never make it. Turn back!'

The roaring of the flames touched their ears.

Fanny could see flashes of angry red showing through the wind-whipped smoke. Her fright grew. She heard Warde's voice. The sudden fear in it drew her sharp look.

'Running along the slope fast as hell . . . getting in behind us!' He pulled at the reins, swung the team out of the road in a sharp turn. The smoke was suddenly thick in the air; made the girl's eyes smart. Warde reached for the whip, slashed at the horses. They jumped forward, cramped a wheel against a boulder. The jar threw Fanny against Warde, and as the frightened horses made another frantic plunge the wheel collapsed with a splintering crash.

Fanny was not sure exactly how she found herself lying sick and dizzy on the ground. She caught a glimpse of the terrified horses on the dead run down the hillside, the wrecked buggy on its side banging at their heels.

Warde limped up, bent over her. 'Hurt?' Panic made his voice hoarse.

She shook her head, scrambled to her feet, ignoring his hand.

Warde spoke again. 'Of all the damn things to happen to me—caught in a forest fire!'

'I'm in this too,' reminded Fanny. She gave him a crooked little smile that was not a smile.

The shaft glanced off him harmlessly. 'Come on!' He seized her by the hand, dragged her along.

Fanny ran stumbling for a few yards. His long

stride was too fast for her, and his grip was hurting her wrist. She broke away from him.

'Stupid of us'—her breath was coming in gasps—'stupid of us to run around in circles.'

Warde halted. 'Want to stand here and burn?' His voice lifted to an angry shout.

'I want to know where I'm running to,' Fanny said quietly. She was surprised at her own coolness. The headache was gone. She had never felt so clearheaded, so in control of her faculties. Warde was shouting at her again. She shook her head, fascinated gaze taking in the sweep of the fire. The changing wind was sending the flames roaring down the lower slopes, away from the green-clad sides of the Palos Verdes. The growth of scrubby piñon, the brush, was like so much tinder.

'No chance to get back by the road we came,' she said. 'We'll be cut off.' She was staring at the bleak, barren ridges lifting in the west. 'Our only chance is over that way, Lester.'

'Unless the wind changes again.' As if under her domination he stood for a few moments, studied the sweep of the fire.

The air was heavy with smoke through which they could glimpse flames licking hungrily at the scrub. Fanny looked again at the barren ridge to the west. Her heart sank. Smoke was spouting up in great geysers from the heavily timbered slope above, and hurled by the wind the flames were already spreading like countless writhing red snakes. It was not going to be possible to reach the high barren ridge in time. Even if they did make through, the dense smoke and scorching heat were not to be endured.

Warde had hold of her hand again, was dragging her along. She went stumblingly, blindly. The smoke choked her every time she drew in a gasping breath. Suddenly she tripped, went down on her face.

The dead weight of her halted Warde. She looked up at him, met his fear-distorted eyes. 'You've got to, you've got to,' he kept telling her. Words refused to come from her parched, smoke-blackened lips. She could only shake her head weakly. It was the end—the end.

Warde suddenly broke off his frantic outburst, stood listening tensely. Sweat glistened on his smoke-begrimed face, gave him a blotchy look. 'Sounds like a voice—somebody calling,' he muttered.

The girl sat up, an extraordinary light in her eyes. 'It *is* somebody—*calling!*' She was suddenly on her feet, screaming. 'Storm—*Storm!*'

Storm was near the turnoff road to the Palos Verdes when he saw the runaway buggy team coming in headlong flight down the hill. Nothing was left of the buggy, save a dangling axle, the hub of a smashed wheel. He knew that team of bays. Lester Warde's buggy team. Warde was proud of those matched bay horses. They were known all over the Little Mesalta.

The fears for the girl that made him leave Mrs. Winston talking to herself and run for his horse took a fresh turn. The moment he had caught the sense of Mrs. Winston's words, Storm understood the meaning of Ed Manners's absence from his office. Manners had learned from the mother that Warde was at the ranch to get Fanny—had followed, to wait in ambush. The man knew Fanny Winston could write his death warrant, was desperately determined to close her mouth in the only way left to him.

Storm made no attempt to puzzle out the meaning of the buggy wreckage trailing at the heels of the runaways. He could only think of Fanny Winston—somewhere up in that raging forest fire. He knew what a forest fire meant, its fearsome, unpredictable fury.

Storm sent the big brown horse up the narrow, twisting road, drew the bandanna around mouth and nose against the smoke that began to engulf him.

He could see scarcely five yards ahead of Cacique's flattened ears. Something loomed in front of them. The brown horse snorted, swerved. The remains of the wrecked buggy. Storm slackened speed. He was close to the scene of the accident. Fanny was not far away. He began to shout. Suddenly, above the crackle and roar of the red

inferno, he faintly caught an answering cry—
Fanny's voice.

Storm swung west from the road, shouted
again. This time the words came clearly. *Storm—
Storm . . . over here.*

He suddenly saw them in the murk, was down
from the horse and lifting the girl into the saddle.
She made no resistance, saw by the quick shake of
his head that he wanted no talk.

A pair of coyotes slithered past them like gray
ghosts in a fog. The brown horse snorted, pawed
nervously. Storm looked at Lester Warde,
motioned for him to climb up behind the girl.

For a fraction of a second hesitation looked from
the lumberman's red-rimmed eyes, then he turned
to obey.

An incoherent cry came from Fanny. Before
Storm could prevent she slid from the saddle.

'I—I'm not going—without you!' She made the
statement simply, with a finality that Storm saw
was unshakable. He looked at her helplessly.

'You're wasting time—and there's none to
waste.' He forced a gruffness that was oddly
tender. There was that in her eyes that made him
tremble.

'Not without you,' Fanny said again.

An animal-like cry burst from Lester Warde. He
was suddenly in the saddle, kicking the horse with
his heels. Cacique sprang forward. In a moment
horse and rider were lost to view in the murk.

Storm halted his frantic spurt to overtake them, ran back to the girl. She met his agonized look with a faint smile. There was no fear in her eyes.

'At least we—we can be together,' she said simply.

Storm took her up, held her close. The feel of her clinging arms was an electrifying shock that roused him to a fury of action. He began to run, still holding her tight against him. A hundred yards or more, then he put her down. 'Come,' he said, 'we're not going to give up.'

The clasp of his hand seemed to pour new strength into Fanny. She felt the power of him, his unconquerable tenacity of purpose. She ran with a sure swiftness that astonished her.

They were making for the same barren ridge that had attracted her attention. Fanny felt a glow of pride. She had been right in seeing the one chance for escape. She would tell Storm—if they ever got out. The fire was crawling fast though, down that wooded hillside above the ridge. Fanny refused to look again, bent her efforts to keep up with the man forging along so steadily.

Storm sensed her growing weariness, heard the quickened breathing. He stopped, gave her a sharp look and picked her up in his arms, was running again.

His strength, his dogged endurance, amazed her. He carried her without visible effort. She could feel the beat of his heart, strong, steady—the heart of a man who could not be beaten.

A bear, followed by two cubs, crashed through the brush ahead of them, tongues lolling. Storm kept on running.

He put her down, looked at her anxiously. Fanny nodded. 'I've got my breath again.'

'The last climb to the ridge,' Storm said. 'We've a chance—a fighting chance—'

They went scrambling up the steep ascent. The smoke rolled in, made her choke. Fanny pulled up the soft pale green skirt, held it to her mouth and nose with her free hand.

Suddenly they were on the summit of the ridge. The girl's heart almost stopped. Below them she could see what looked like a great black river that reached into the distance between stunted pine trees.

For the moment they were fairly free from the smoke, but the fire was racing down the wooded slope, would soon be savagely attacking the pines in the canyon below.

Fanny's distressed face turned to Storm. He seemed undisturbed, in fact strangely cheerful.

'That's a lava bed, down there,' he said. 'Come on!' He clasped her hand and they started down the hill. It was slippery work. Fanny gritted her teeth, held on to Storm. A cliff suddenly confronted them.

'I can't do it,' Fanny almost wept. She was breathing with difficulty.

'Yes, you can,' Storm said. He lowered her by

her hands, let go of her. It was a short fall. She landed safely on both feet. Storm slid down, stared quickly about at their surroundings.

They were on the lava bed. It looked like a great river boiling up in black waves.

'Should be somewhere close,' Storm said half to himself. He took her in his arms again, moved a few yards across the black lava flow, came to a standstill. Fanny was suddenly aware of a delicious chill on her face. A wild thought came to her. She was going mad.

Storm put her down carefully, warned her to watch her step. The lava was knife-sharp, could cut her shoes to ribbons.

Somewhat in a daze she obeyed his gesture, crawled through a narrow opening that gaped in the black rock. She had to go down on her hands and knees to squeeze inside. Something cold crushed under her hands. Snow! Fanny decided she was not *going* mad, she was already mad, imagining the most absurd things.

She felt Storm crawling to her side, heard his voice, cheerful, exultant. 'Lucky I remembered this place.'

The miracle of the thing, the relief, had its way with her. She had kept up her courage to the amazing end, and now the letdown came. She began to cry softly, head against his shirtsleeve. 'I—I'm co-cold—freezing—'

'You would be.' Storm's tone was amused.

'You're in an ice cave.' He put an arm around her, drew her close, gave her his warmth.

Fanny was silent for a long moment, and then, 'I wonder if Lester got away.'

'I hope my horse did,' Storm answered shortly.

Warde was leaving it to the brown horse. Terror dogged Cacique's heels. He found the road, went down the grade at a wild gallop. The man on his back clung to saddlehorn. A fall meant the finish. He was not going to fall. His long legs clamped tight in a desperate hold.

The fire was licking into the scrub near the intersection. The horse swerved, made for a stretch of bare ground, and was suddenly in the Mesalta road.

Warde let out a yell, flogged the lathered flanks. The tired horse shook his head in protest, slowed down to a jog. Warde failed to see the man crouching in the scrub. Smoke was drifting across the road like misting fog, and his eyes were smarting.

Ed Manners's thin lips twisted in triumph as he watched the slowly jogging horse. He couldn't see very clearly either through the smoke drift. But he could see enough to recognize Storm MacKenzie's horse. Lester Warde hadn't come along with the girl from the ranch yet, but here was Storm MacKenzie—an unsuspecting victim.

Manners lifted the rifle—fired, saw the rider collapse in the saddle, go plunging to the road. The brown horse snorted, started to run, slowed to a standstill as four riders tore down the winding grade. Manners heard them, went scrambling through the piñons to his concealed horse. A gunshot crashed out and the murderer halted. His legs wouldn't move, were locked in a paralyzing grip of fright.

Dave Stagg took one look at the brown horse, standing there, head hanging, legs trembling from exhaustion. 'Stormy's horse!' His voice was a despairing groan. He ran to the man lying in the road, uttered a loud yell. 'Ain't Stormy! It's Warde—layin' here!'

Pete Kendall and Yuma were dragging the horrified Manners from the scrub. Dave turned from the dead man, stared at the quailing prisoner. 'Was Storm MacKenzie's horse, all right, but the man ridin' him weren't Stormy.' Doom was in Dave's voice. 'You'll swing just the same Ed—swing for killin' Warde.'

The rain began gently in the higher hills, was suddenly a quenching downpour. Storm looked out, saw the big drops pelting the hard black lava. He was not surprised. Only that morning he had looked across at the lofty San Franciscos, seen the 'clouds smokin'.' The old tradition was still working.

He helped the shivering girl out of the cave.

Fanny lifted her face to the dripping sky. 'It's wet,' she said, 'but it's warmer than in that place.' Her look went wonderingly to the cave. 'Something to do with volcanic action—ages ago, I suppose.'

Storm nodded. He was not interested in the ice cave. His thoughts were on the girl, standing there in the rain, bedraggled, smoke-begrimed—more than ever radiantly alive.

Fanny grew conscious of his look. 'I must be a sight!' Her tone was rueful. 'Your mother's dress is ruined.'

Storm shook his head, reached out and drew her close. Fanny made no resistance. 'I'm an awfully wet little thing,' was all she said. Her face lifted, eyes tender. 'You look so serious, Storm.'

'I'm thinking of something Ynes was saying to me, the day you came in on the Flagstaff stage.'

'What did Ynes say, Storm?' Fanny's eyes were suddenly shy.

'She said she was praying for me to find a nice girl—bring her home to the Diamond M.' Storm's voice was not quite steady. 'Last night she told me her prayers were answered with a miracle—that *you* are the miracle.'

They stood there, heedless of the smouldering hills—the beating rain. The world was drawn very close around them, in the eyes of each a glory and a vision.

Center Point Publishing
600 Brooks Road ● PO Box 1
Thorndike ME 04986-0001 USA

(207) 568-3717

**US & Canada:
1 800 929-9108**
www.centerpointlargeprint.com